Diary of a 6th Grade

Book 1 –

Zero to Hero

Fantasy Books for Kids

Katrina Kahler

Copyright © KC Global Enterprises Pty Ltd

All Rights Reserved

Table of Contents

Chapter 1 - The Library...

The doors of the library slide open with a gentle swish. There is a hushed silence as I walk inside. If I stand still I can feel there are soft whispers of secrets being told. I walk in slowly hoping no one will notice me. My plan is to tiptoe past the library counter and hand in my books. Then I want to disappear into the peace and quiet of the book shelves. Story books, travel books, tales of ancient civilizations - all amazing places to escape to. This is the best place for a 'latch- key kid' to spend the afternoon. Mom and dad work hard to send me to Bedford View Primary but then they are so busy that I hardly ever see them. Today mom is working late again! The library is the spot for me, Samuel Greene, to spend the afternoon.

I draw in a deep breath and walk up to the librarian's desk. I hope Miss Sorrel is in a good mood today. I wonder why our previous librarian left so suddenly. She just disappeared one afternoon. Nobody knows where she went. I miss her; she was really nice and so kind.

Miss Sorrel doesn't like me! She makes fun of my rather long name. My full name had to include my grandfather's and great grandfather's names. It is a mouthful. Five names to remember – Samuel, Peter, Rupert, Orpen-Greene. Miss Sorrel looked at my library card on her first day as the new librarian, leaned over the counter, and said, "Your initials spell S.P.R.O-G - Sprog…just the right name for YOU - little boy!"

I remember that day well. I heard some giggling in the background and then Abigail came to my rescue. She told Miss Sorrel that my real name is Sam, Sam Greene. Miss Sorrel looked down her nose at me and glared into my eyes. I remember feeling very small at that very moment. Miss Sorrel makes me feel nervous.

I always try to ease quietly into the library now and go unnoticed. But Miss Sorrel just appears from nowhere and grins at me.

She delights in taking my card and mutters my name under her breath.

When I look up I see a long hair on her chin and a rather large Adam's apple. Today, Miss Sorrel takes my library cards and gives me a library browsing stick to keep a record of where I have taken a book. She has a firm grip on the end of the stick and I see that her nails are very dirty. I wonder if she remembers to wash her hands before reading a book! One of the rules of the library!

Relieved to be past the front desk I set off into the book shelves. On the way, I take a quick look at the 'Readathon' results. I have been doing well as I am a good reader and like books, but what a disappointment! I see my marker is down to zero again. I wonder how that can be. Last time I challenged Miss Sorrel she said in a deep voice, "The wind blew your name down! Sorry for you - you're back to zero again!"

 Again! That is so unfair, but I am too nervous to remind her that I was at the top of the class list. I can't tell Miss Sorrel that she is wrong. Who knows how she may react.

It is going to be a long afternoon but I have a small snack pack in my pocket. Some sweets left over from the movie we went to last night. Jungle book in 3D - it was amazing. One of my favorite stories! I wonder for a moment what it would be like to be raised by wolves. Then I remember what I am really looking for. The plant section of the library, I wish I had paid more attention to the system used to number the books. Well, I know plants are part of botanical books so that's where I shall start. Right in the middle of the library.

My Mom has started a cooking course and needs fresh herbs. If I can grow them in the back yard that will be a great help. There must be a book about herbs and how to grow them.

Not many children come to this part of the library and I have a sense that I am being followed. Each time I turn around to see who it could be…the passage is empty. A very uneasy feeling comes over me. I hurry along now to the shelves where all the books about plants are. I hope I can find just the right book and make my way back to the front of the library as soon as possible.

Aahhh, here are the books about plants. I can see not many children have been down to this part of the library. The books about herbs seem to be on the top shelf so, with the help of a little stool, I stand up to reach for a book called 'How to grow your own Herbs'. I am just putting my browsing stick up to mark the spot when I lose my balance. The stool wobbles under me and I tumble down to the ground. Before I can get up another book falls down from the top together with my browser stick. They fall on my head and I feel dizzy. Then the space around me starts to twist and turn and I lose sight of where I am. I seem to be going round and round as if I am on a roundabout. Finally, the roundabout stops and I rub my eyes and my head. I feel strange. I can't see any books near me but I am still a little dazed and can't see clearly. Perhaps some dust is in my eyes from the dusty bookshelves. I rub my eyes again but the picture I see is still not clear.

Suddenly, I have a brain wave. I wonder if my mom packed the 3D glasses from the movies. They were part of the kiddie's combo I had for my snack. Bingo! There they are still wrapped in plastic. Slowly and carefully I put them on! WOW, it is just like being at a 3D movie. The whole picture in front of me comes alive – like magic! I just stare around at the scene and my mouth opens wide. I gasp! There is not a book in sight. How can that be, what has happened to me?

I am sitting on the grass looking at a beautiful garden and a long path leading to a castle.

If I am not in the library right now then where am I?

Chapter 2 – Gardinia...

Questions are buzzing through my mind about where I am and how did I get here? What has happened to the library? The only thing I have with me from the library is the browser stick and my 3D glasses. Another look round the scene tells me I am definitely not in the library.

Wait a minute, something is walking down the path and it is coming towards me! I squint through the glasses again and see that the creature coming towards me is a wolf.

For real! A large, white, wolf.

A flash-back image to the movie I saw reminds me that animals bow down to more important or stronger animals - the leader of a wolf pack is no exception.

I bow down really low and wait, holding my breath. After what seems like hours (well maybe minutes) I feel the hot breath of an animal on my back and hear the sounds of the wolf sniffing. He sniffs me from top to toe. I wait, trembling and not sure of what will happen to me.

Finally, I hear a low growl and a voice says, "Welcome to Gardinia, I can tell that you are a friend. You smell good."

Oh no, how crazy is this I think to myself. There is a wolf, a huge white wolf, talking to me!

Curiosity gets the better of me and I lift my head up slowly and respectfully. I see I am looking up into the face of a wolf. It has a kindly expression and beautiful eyes, but it talks!! How can that be? I must be dreaming. I take the 3D glasses on and off a couple of times but without them, I can only see a few blurry outlines. The 3D glasses allow me to see this place the wolf calls Gardinia.

 Gardinia looks rather neglected but must have been beautiful once. What a lovely name.

Now what! I think to myself. How do I answer a wolf? I clear my throat and say.

"Err it is nice to meet you, Mr Wolf. My name is Sam, Sam Greene and I got here by accident."

Wow, how weird is that! Me - talking to a wolf. Maybe these 3D glasses are more powerful than I thought. Thank goodness mom forgot to take them out of my movie treat box.

"My name is Cannis Lupis Arctos," says the wolf. "You can call me Lupa. I am chief of the home-guard in Gardinia. Why are you here?"

"Well actually I was looking for some information on growing herbs," I answered quietly. "I want to help my mom have fresh herbs in her garden and I was in the library at school and suddenly I found myself here in your beautiful land." I think saying nice things is a good idea even if this wolf looks friendly and kind, he is still a wolf!

"You have actually come at a bad time," says Lupa. "Our beautiful land is feeling the sorrow of the King and Queen of Gardinia. There is a dark shadow creeping over the land and we do not know how to control it." "Grrrrrr..." he growls under his breath.

"The worst sadness of all is Princess Gazania, the King and Queen's only daughter has been missing for several days. No one knows where she could be. Princess Gazania just disappeared without a trace."

Oh no, disappearing, that sounds familiar. I wonder

if there is a connection between our missing librarian and the lost Princess. Oh and my disappearing readathon points I should be at the top of the chart by now.

I want to talk to Lupa a bit more but he beckons with his head for me to follow him along the road towards the castle. Walking slowly next to him I feel safe and look around at the gardens and the path leading to the castle. There is something missing from the sounds of the garden and the feeling of deep sorrow surrounds everything. There are a few flowers but their heads are bowed down and their color seems rather dull.

"What season it is in Gardinia right now? " I ask Lupa.

"It should be summer," he tells me. "but we are not getting the sunshine we need. Clouds are coming over from the dark side. Then for some reason, the bees that used to pollinate our flowers are not coming to the gardens. Summer was always filled with buzzing bees and bright colors. We were so grateful for summertime. Many bees have left their hives, and their honey and pollen have gone too."

The castle steps are in front of us and we are walking up them before I get a chance to discuss the importance of bees. There are two rows of white wolves standing on either side of the steps and as we walk up they bow down with respect to their leader Lupa. I walk with Lupa up the steps and have an uneasy sense of being watched and checked by the wolf guard. Lupa growls under his breath and I presume he is telling the wolves that I am a good person, not to be feared.

At the top of the stairs, we are met by an old man with a very long beard.

He bangs on the floor and all the wolves lie down. Wow, that was so cool...but I am glad I am with Lupa and considered to be a friend.

The man with the beard says, "Who goes there?"

"Sam Greene, a visitor to see the King," says Lupa

with confidence.

"On what business?" asks the old man.

"He comes to seek advice on growing herbs," says Lupa. "I have brought him to meet the King."

"Hummmmm," the old man looks up at the sky and down to the ground and towards the castle and finally he says, "That may be a good diversion for the King, he loves to talk about his gardens."

The old man bangs on the floor again and the door opens to reveal the large entrance hall and opening into the castle. Lupa leads the way and we walk into the King's castle...the castle of Gardinia.

We are on our way to meet the King and I can hardly take all this in. Is it all for real? I pinch my arm and confirm that this is really happening to me. Soon we will meet the King of Gardinia.

Lupa indicates with a nod of his head again that I should bow my head when I meet the King.

Lupa introduces me and we wait for the King to look up and acknowledge us. Slowly the King does so but he looks tired and very, very sad.

I feel really sorry for him. He must be terribly worried about his daughter, Gazania. I am sure the last thing he wants to talk about is herbs.

"Welcome," says the King and with a wave of his royal arm, he invites us to sit by his throne. The conversation is difficult as the King keeps trailing off and forgetting what he is saying. Lupa gets up and I follow his lead. It is time to leave.

We make our way out of the castle and follow the path outside into the gardens.

I feel the dark clouds gathering in the sky and there is an air of gloom over the land. I am very nervous.

It is time to go but how do I get back to the library? Oh and there's Uncle Bert! My mom's brother was coming for dinner and he will be waiting to get into the flat. Reality check!

Lupa seems to read my mind.

"I can sense you need to get home," he says with a sigh. "You are a brave boy, I wish you could stay and help us solve our problems. We need someone like you from the outside world who is clever and courageous."

I am honored a large white arctic wolf is calling me brave. Ha, I wish Miss Sorrel could see me now!

Suddenly a large winged creature flies by and just misses my head! The sun is going down and the light is getting dimmer. What was that creature? A bat? No, it wasn't quite big enough...maybe a night owl. No, too early for owls.

Lupa looks worried and pulls his ears back. The sound comes back again and this time there are two of them. Winged creatures making a terrible whirring sound with their wings, I am sure I even heard one squeak.

"What was that Lupa?" I ask with a tremble in my voice.

"We think they are giant moths that have come from the dark side but no one is sure. They are very scary as they dive at your head and squeak like bats but we know they are not bats. Everyone goes inside at night, the people of Gardinia are afraid."

Giant moths that squeak like bats! Suddenly I am afraid too. It really is time to go!

We have reached the place where I landed several hours ago. So much has happened and my head is buzzing with stories of giant moths and the dark side of Gardinia. Lupa is anxious to return to the castle too.

"Do you have the stick you arrived with?" he asks.

The browsing stick from the library is tucked into my belt a bit like a sword. I take it out to show Lupa and as I hold it up in the air everything turns upside down again and I spin round and round. I feel the falling sensation. I gasp for breath and find myself sitting on the library floor again.

Back where I started.

I pick myself up feeling a bit dazed but no broken bones. The sound of the home-time bell rings in the background. A quick dash takes me to the front of the library. Careful not to draw any attention to myself I leave the library silently. I'm anxious to get home and think about the afternoon I spent in Gardinia.

I hope Uncle Bert hasn't been waiting too long. Mom's brother was a forensic entomologist. He helped the police detectives find clues to crimes through the bugs and beetles that were on the crime scene. What a cool job. He doesn't like to talk much about the work he did. Kind of secret police work but sometimes he has something interesting to say. Mom says he's too clever for one he should have been twins!

Perhaps Uncle Bert may have something to say about giant moths.

Chapter 3 – Decisions, Decisions...

I arrive breathless at the door. Uncle Bert is there waiting on the patio. Apologizing, I let him into the house to have his cup of tea and some telly before Mom and Dad arrive. He seems to be in a good mood and I am glad that I can scoot off to my room and take in all that happened today.

Wow, what an amazing experience! I am still in shock from the idea of being able to travel into a different place through the pages of a book in the library! And, how about meeting a wolf, an enormous white wolf that talks to me. The memory of walking to the castle door through an avenue of wolves, the castle guard, is just the best.

But some memories are not so good. I shudder when I think of the distraught King who has lost his only daughter. I never met the Queen – she is too sad to leave her room. There seems to be unrest in the land. A force of evil that is part of the darkness and shadows that are creeping closer towards the castle. Shadows lurk there and are not explained. The plants are dying and what has happened to the bees. A garden cannot function without bees! The wolf was clearly afraid of the giant moths that dived out of the evening sky. People don't want to come out after dark. Something is not right, but without knowing the full story what can I do? There is a lot to think about.

"Sam, supper time," calls Mom.

Oh good. I am starving! This could be my chance to see what Uncle Bert knows about giant moths.

I rush downstairs and sit next to Uncle Bert. I am waiting for the right moment to ask him about moths. Just before pudding, I think. Uncle Bert likes to get on with his first course without interruptions. He is very particular about his food.

"Err-um," I clear my throat and ask politely, "Excuse me, Uncle Bert, do you know anything about giant moths, I mean really big ones?"

Uncle Bert looks up from his bowl of ice-cream and says, "Yes, young Sam, I do. There are a number of really large moths. The largest in the world is the Atlas moth and then there are Lunar moths. They are very beautiful. The American dagger moth is an interesting one."

Uncle Bert pauses for a moment and continues with a more serious voice.

"But I think the most fascinating is the Death's Head Hawk moth. I remember a case I had with a dark side to the investigation and....

"Thanks, Uncle Bert," Mom interrupts and says, "I think we will leave out the details of that one. It might be a little bit too scary for Sam just before bedtime!"

Mom changes the conversation to ask about the Readathon and school and a few other things that I answer easily while still thinking about giant moths. I will do my own investigation, I tell myself. In the library tomorrow I will look under butterflies and moths, biology I guess.

I say goodnight to everyone and go to my room knowing that I will not be going off to sleep easily. I have to decide if I will help Lupa and go back to Gardinia. It seems like a big task for one person but I am the only one involved right now.

Morning time arrives and the alarm goes off as normal.

Getting ready for school is part of a daily routine and I am actually glad that Mom wants me to stay late again. When I woke up this morning I knew that I had to try and get back to Gardinia and at least try and understand the full story of what is happening there. I pack my bag and make sure that I have my 3D glasses so that if I do find the way into the book I will be able to see my way around and connect with Lupa. Maybe I will meet some other Gardinians and together we can understand why the land is being taken over by some dark force and what has happened to Princess Gazania.

The school morning is very boring. There isn't a single lesson that really makes me feel excited about learning. The library is the place I want to be right now, but I have to wait for the afternoon. The library opens for studying and homework from 2 pm. That's when I will have to go in and try to get past Miss Sorrel and into the Botany section of the library. I hope I can find the right book again to get me back to Gardinia.

My friend Abs keeps waving at me from across the room. I try to avoid her gaze and arms waving. She is reminding me about chess this afternoon. I wave back and say silently that I am sorry I am not able to play. She wants to know why but I just shake my head and say sorry. I like Abs but she is a bit nosey!

The bell rings, time to leave and set off to the library. I am feeling good about my decision and excited to be going back to Gardinia. I need to get past Miss Sorrel as quickly as I can and collect my book browser stick. Then I will be set. I am not even going to check the Readathon results as I have more important things to do now.

I walk into the library with 'walking feet' as our previous librarian had told us. Rather a babyish expression but it did work. I took my 'walking feet' to the counter and waited quietly for Miss Sorrel. She leaned over the counter in her usual abrupt fashion and said,

"Oh, it's SPRO-G again. The tiny little boy from Grade 6. Let me have a better look at you."

She leaned over the counter and once again I saw her a hair on her chin and big Adams' apple. Her gruff voice began to say something when her glasses fell off her nose. I bent to help her pick them up. She did so at the same time. Our faces met around the side of the library counter. Getting up close to Miss Sorrel was a scary experience. Her eyes were dark and looked right into me as if she knew everything about me. Her fingers were so boney and long as she reached out for her glasses. Then as she was leaning forward her scarf fell from around her neck. Before she could put it back I saw a tattoo on her neck. A real tattoo, not that licky-sticky kind you get at some kid's parties. A tattoo for real and it looked like a skull. The sign of evil or bad omen. I am pretty sure Miss Sorrel is not who we think she is. I am busy wondering who she is when she straightens up and puts her scarf where it should be. She is hiding the tattoo and who knows what else. A job for Uncle Bert maybe, he is good at solving mysteries. I have no time for guessing games so I grab my browser stick and disappear as quickly as possible.

Down the aisles I go to get back to the herb section. I need 'How to grow your own Herbs'. I am in such a hurry. Someone is following me but there is no time to turn and see who it is. There is definitely someone else close by. Maybe in the same aisle with me. I brush off the uneasy feeling that I have because I need to concentrate right now to get back to Gardinia. I try to repeat the actions from yesterday in my mind. Firstly I found the book I wanted, then I tried to reach it with a stool, I used my browser stick to reach the space where the book was. I try to repeat those actions. Yes! I am on the right track.

I start to spin and fall off the stool. Round and round I go and suddenly the spinning stops and I land on the ground in Gardinia. I catch my breath and look around.

This is Gardinia. I put my 3D glasses on and deliberately put my browser into my belt like a sword. Now I know it has a special function. I am looking around hoping Lupa will be close by. I see him walking down the road in the same way that he did before. A kind of lope and sadly with his head hanging low. He is worried about many things and the happiness of this land. It should be a wonderful place enjoying the midsummer days. I bow down low as Lupa arrives and he greets me, "Welcome Sam Greene, Gardinia is so glad to see you back again"

"Thank you, Lupa," I reply. "I am glad I managed to get back to see you again. I have so many questions to ask you."

Together we walk towards the castle and as we go along the path I think of all the things I need to ask Lupa about this land called Gardinia.

Lupa leads me to a bench in the garden and indicates with his head that I should sit. I sit and he sits by me on the grass. Lupa nods his head and says, "Ask your questions and I hope I can answer. There are many mysterious things happening that no one can understand."

I decide to start with the King and his family. The King must be the key to so many things surrounding the history of Gardinia.

"Tell me about the King," I ask Lupa.

"Perhaps I should tell you a story," says Lupa. I nod and start to listen.

"Once there was a King who lived in a castle with his brother. The King was a man of peace and loved his garden. His name was Rhizome and his brother was called Rumex. The two brothers had a good life in the castle and were raised to love plants. Rumex loved herbs and unusual plants and Rhizome loved garden flowers and exotic bulbs. The boys grew up and married. Rhizome had a son, Costus. When King Rhizome he died his son, now King Costus, became the new King of Gardinia. Rumex or Uncle Ru as he was known became very jealous. His wife was jealous too as they had no children. They decided to build their own castle on the other side of the river and they moved away. The land of Gardinia became divided. King Costus Of Gardinia has a beautiful daughter he called Gazania meaning treasure. She is his treasure. Uncle Ru became more jealous and furious. He has no children and he will never be King. The sad thing about this story is there is no Princess left to live happily ever after and no King to reign happily ever after."

"I am so sorry Lupa, the story is very sad. There are a lot of other confusing things besides the story though. Can you answer some questions for me?"

Lupa bows his head, "I'll try my best."

"I need to know something about the dark side over the river. The shadows and whispers that come from the forest. The castle that is barely visible on the far hill. Then on this side of Gardinia why are there so few plants and bees? Why are the people so afraid? And the biggest question of all, where do the giant moths come from?" I asked, questions quickly flowing from my mouth.

Lupa's eyes looked sad. "Yes, we have many problems. We need help before our land dies and the dark side takes over. We need to restore love, kindness, and goodness. While the King's daughter is missing he has no love to share with his people. Without love, there is no goodness and kindness. Will you help us? Help us find the King's daughter and restore this land of Gardinia to it real beauty and glory?" Lupa asked.

I cannot resist the plea from the wolf. I am sure I see a tear escape from his eyes.

"Yes Lupa, I will help you," I say, but I wonder if I can do this alone. It is a huge challenge!

I need to go home and come up with a plan. Look at some clues and see what resources I have. I decide to come back and start to trace the steps Gazania took before she was kidnapped.

"I must go Lupa, but I will return and plan what to do. We will find the King's daughter," I say confidently.

I say farewell and with a wave of my browser stick and a whizzing sound, I whirl back to the library. I land with a bump at the bottom of the bookcase where I left from. At that moment I realize that I am not alone, someone is sitting on the stool that I had used to reach the top shelf. Someone is staring at me!

Chapter 4 - Little Miss Nosey Parker...

I landed with a thump and looked straight into the big blue eyes of Abigail Hartley.

She gasped and her eyes bulged with a look of great disbelief.

I was shocked to see her there and wondered if she had any idea of what I was involved in.

"Abs," I say, trying not to sound too nervous. "What are you doing in this part of the library?"

"I want to ask you the same question!" says Abs.

"I've been following you for the last two days and something weird is going on." And she blurts out, "You never miss a chess game. I want to know what you are up to Sam Greene!"

"Well it's private," I answer quickly as I don't want to give out any information. It is all too weird even for me and how will I explain it all to Abs?

Abs gets all offended and pouts there and then.

"Well if you won't tell me...then I am going to tell on you!" she says crossly.

I think to myself that she is using bribery and being very childish! But what can I do, she has caught me in the middle of something I can't explain unless I include her in the secret. I don't want to cause a scene in the library, so I say quietly, "Okay Abs I will tell you what is happening. It is exciting and scary all at the same time. You have to promise not to say a word. You also have to leave the library right now and meet me at my house this afternoon. Pretend that we are going to study together and we are working on a project. I can't tell you anything here. I need you to leave right now and let me follow separately so that no one sees us leaving together."

Abs nods, I can see she is super excited about being part of the secret that I am going to share with her.

Abigail is very bright, top of the class and a very

good chess player. It is difficult to fool Abs. I will have to think very carefully about how I tell her about Gardina and the mysterious disappearance of Gazania. Perhaps it will be a good idea to have another pair of eyes and ears on the case.

I sound a bit like Uncle Bert now, referring to the problem as a case, but then this is an investigation! If Abs joins forces with me perhaps we will have a better chance of finding Gazania. We need to find her soon and we need to find who is trying to harm the land of Gardina and why.

I try to get out of the library unnoticed but Miss Sorrel is waiting for me. She glares down her nose at me as I try to pass by the desk. Her nostrils flare and I feel very uncomfortable.

She makes a loud sniff and then a sneeze and then a sniff again.

"You smell musty, dusty like a dirty garden." She sniffs again. "Like a dry pathway in a dry garden."

I shudder a bit and try not to look stressed. How does she know so much? It is as if she has a second sense and I don't like the way she is sniffing me. Surely that's not normal for a grown woman!

"'Sorry Miss Sorrel, it's nothing," I say quickly. "Must be some dust on my shoes."

I dash out of the library without a backward glance

and rush home so I can get there before Abigail. I want to tidy my room before she gets here, it is a mess!

A knock on the front door tells me Abs has arrived. Mom and Dad are not home yet so I run downstairs. "Hi Abs, thanks for coming over and not making a fuss today," Abs smirks.

Our home is small but comfortable. It is not as grand as some of the other homes that the Bedford View children come from, but it is just right for our family.

I take Abs upstairs to my room where I study and have my desk.

"This is where I do my work so when my mom comes home she will be glad we are studying together and getting our homework done. I think we should tell her we are working on a project together.

Abs nods her head but I can see she just wants to hear what I have discovered in the library. "Okay Sam, spit it out, what are you up to?"

"Abs," I say very quietly and seriously. "'What I am about to tell you has to stay between us. It is confidential. LIVES ARE AT STAKE!"

Abigail nods ever so seriously, raises her eyebrows and waits to hear more.

"You may not believe this, but I promise you, it is all true and really happened to me. There are some scary things going on and I can't explain anything yet. I think our library is in DANGER too!"

When I see I have her undivided attention...I tell Abs about going to the land of Gardinia, through a passage of time, in a book. That's the best way to explain what happened. Then I tell her about the wolf, the King and his castle and everything else I can remember. Suddenly it feels good to talk to someone else.

Abigail is a good listener and her eyes look sad when I say how distraught the King and Queen are at losing their daughter. "That is such a sad story Sam, we have to help!"

Finally when I tell her about the giant moths she shivers and wrinkles up her nose in disbelief.

Finally, I finish telling her everything and let out a sigh of relief. I think she is going to laugh or call me a liar or a story-teller. She does nothing like that. She looks me square in the eyes and says, "Oh Sam, this is urgent, we have to help find Princess Gazania. We need to look at all the clues and try to trace her last steps to see how she disappeared."

"Abs, I'm so relieved you believe me. I was worried you might think I had gone totally bonkers! I couldn't have a better friend as an investigator on my team."

"What about the library Sam?" she asks. "You said the library was in danger too. What did you mean by that?"

Abs amazes me, she doesn't miss much. I had not told her about the library but she remembered that it was part of the problem. I explain that I am very unsure of my suspicions but they revolve around Miss Sorrel and the fact that our real librarian left without a word. I don't like Miss Sorrel, and she does not like me. I feel I have to warn Abs that I have my suspicions. If we are going to be partners in this crime investigation then we need to be honest with each other.

"'Okay Abs, it's time to think how we can start to solve this case."

I feel very important when I call it a criminal investigation. A bit like Uncle Bert and his stories of crime scene investigations. How did he organize his team? I try to remember and to think of the hundreds of TV shows I have watched while waiting for mom and dad to come home.

"'First we need to have a board up with all the characters involved and anything we know about them. One we can add to as we get more information. Uncle Bert says every little detail is important." I can see Abs nodding and taking all this in carefully.

"A bit like a storyboard," she says. "We did one in

class the other day before we wrote our stories. It helps with the planning."

I can see Abs is really trying to be helpful. I have a board in my room to pin-up my favorite posters. Mom doesn't want me to stick things on the wall or the cupboards. It will be perfect for planning and writing as we get our information. We decide to use a code for the names so if my Mom comes in and reads what we have written, she won't know what it is about. We decide on a pictured storyboard with a flower representing Gazania in the middle.

The rest of the afternoon went by in a flash as we put up all the names and picture clues of every other person or animal that is part of the investigation. I had to tell Abs the persons, animals and places that were important. She carefully made picture clues for each part of the investigation. In the end, we had a board full of all sorts of characters that were from Gardinia. We knew there was a connection to the library but that connection was not clear yet.

Just as Abs was about to speak, the doorbell rang and I knew it was Uncle Bert. He comes over three times a week for a bit of supper.

"Time to go Abs," I say. "I will let you out and see you at school tomorrow. Remember not a word about this to anyone. We need to continue this investigation on our own."

Abigail nods and I show her out of the house. I walk back inside and see Uncle Bert sitting quietly in the lounge. His favorite TV show has not started yet.

I walk over to him and ask a quick question about investigating a crime. "Hi Uncle Bert," I say cheerfully. "I am doing a project on being a detective and I want to ask you a few questions. Is that okay?"

"Sure," says Uncle Bert. "As long as your mother is not here, she gets very angry if I talk about my time as a detective. She prefers to hear about the entomology in the jungle!"

Uncle Bert chuckles and I see that I have a chance to ask something that will help Abs and I, the two detectives. I tell Uncle Bert about a project we are doing together and ask him what the most important part of the investigation is."

Uncle Bert thinks for a moment and says, "The crime scene investigation! You must go back to the scene of the crime as soon as possible and gather all the evidence that you can. Then interview anyone who had anything to do with the crime. Even if you think they are innocent – suspect everyone and dig deep for your information. Leave no stone unturned," he says in a very serious voice.

I have a little chuckle to myself as the investigation is taking place in a garden and there will be many stones to turn and look at. What will creep out from under the stones and rocks? We will have to go back to Gardinia once more but this time with a purpose.

Crime scene investigators ready, willing and able.

Chapter 5 - Crime Scene Investigation...

The school bell rings and everyone lines up ready to go into their classes. "Psst.," whispers Abigail. She is dying to talk to me but I silence her with a stare and she nods and turns away looking very innocent. We cannot be seen talking to each other and from now on we must act like undercover cops.

I pass Abigail in the passage and slip her a note.

Meet me in the library
this afternoon.
Bring 3D glasses if you
have some and a
notebook.

Next time I see Abs she gives me a thumbs-up and so I know she has got the message. We will meet in the library and sneak down to the Botany section. I am not sure if we will both get into Gardinia but I have to hope that what worked for me will work for

Abs. Otherwise, I am on the crime scene by myself.

The library doors are open for afternoon study groups and avid readers who want to change their books. I look at the Readathon chart as I go in. My name tag has not moved up and I know I returned all my books last week. I am still at zero!

Miss Sorrel is waiting at the librarian's counter but she is not really focused on the children wanting to change their books. Her attention is taken up by gazing at a strange creature she has on the counter. She gazes at a glass jar that is upside down and full of leaves. A large and brightly colored caterpillar is munching the leaves. Miss Sorrel clucks and tuts like a mother hen over the rather ugly, creepy caterpillar. Its bright shades of green, blue and yellow are beautiful, but it has an ugly horn at the end of its body and an ugly sort of mouth to chomp at the leaves. It reminds me in a way of Beauty and the Beast.

Most of the girls are making strange noises like "eeewe" and "gross" and they keep their distance from the library counter. Boys, on the other hand, are fascinated by this brightly colored creature and are getting close to the glass jar. I decide to join the boys and get closer to the jar to catch a glimpse of Miss Sorrels 'pet'. As I look over someone's shoulder in front of me, the caterpillar stands up on its back legs and tries to gnash at the jar with what looks like kind of pincers. Abs tells me after wards they are mandibles and can bite if you get close enough.

Miss Sorrel continues to be totally in awe of the caterpillar and so I signal to Abs to pick out her browser stick and follow me to the Botany section of the library. I am hoping that what worked for me will work for Abs and we can both travel to Gardinia together. I feel excited and nervous at the same time. I am busy concentrating on my plan for the investigation when I bump into Abs who is waiting round the corner of the Botany aisle. We both get a fright and gasp but manage to keep in control of our mutual excitement.

"Okay Abs," I whisper, "We need to find the book called 'How to grow your own Herbs'. That's the book I was trying to get out of the library. Then we must put out our browsers as if we are going to take that book off the shelf."

Abigail nods with a serious look on her face. I can

see she is concentrating very hard and I'm actually glad that she is coming with me this time.

"I think if we stand on the stool together and you put your arms around my waist we should be taken up to Gardinia together. Have you brought your 3D glasses?"

I can feel Abs nod behind me as she wraps her arms around my waist. Clearly, this is not a time to be thinking about a girl having her arms around my waist!

"Hold on tight, close your eyes and away we go!"

Suddenly the library whirls round and round and with a mighty whoosh we are lifted up and land with a bump in Gardinia.

"Abs," I call out, "Are you here? Are you okay?"

I am so relieved when I hear a rather shaky voice reply.

"Yes, I am fine. Just a bit dizzy and I can't seem to focus on anything," says Abs.

"Put your 3D glasses on and see what happens."

Suddenly I hear a gasp of surprise from behind me and I know it is Abigail. She has put on the 3D glasses and Gardinia has come to life in front of her.

Abs crawls over to sit next to me and together we look up the path leading to the castle.

This is our crime scene and we need to have a plan of action. Abs, has her notebook out, "Sam, I've listed all the people and animals we need to talk to." I am impressed.

The list starts with Lupa and as I am looking at his name I see that he is walking down the path towards us. "Abs, Lupa is the leader of the guard and we need to greet him with respect."

I bow down and Abs copies me. We wait for Lupa to acknowledge us.

I did not have time to prepare Abs for the sniffing process but she is very brave and keeps still while Lupa makes sure she is a friend.

"Welcome friends," says Lupa. "I see you have brought someone with you, Sam. An addition to your pack. Always a good idea to have some help, what is your friend's name?"

"Her name is Abigail, Abs for short." They bow to each other and I know Lupa has accepted Abs as a fellow helper and friend.

"Lupa, we are here as crime scene investigators. We need to be able to talk to anyone who knew Princess Gazania and can remember anything important before she disappeared," I say in a serious tone.

Abs reads out some of the names on her list. Lupa is shocked to hear his name! "Why is my name on that list Sam? Surely you don't think I would ever harm the Princess!" said Lupa.

"Trust us, Lupa, this is how crimes are solved. We must investigate thoroughly. Just remember that everyone is innocent before proven guilty." This is a useful expression that I had picked up from Uncle Bert.

Lupa fur lowered on his spine, he seemed to

understand that we were not picking on him. "Come follow me," says Lupa.

Together we follow Lupa and I can see Abs staring in wonder at everything. "Isn't it beautiful Abs," I say to her, but she hardly hears me, her eyes looked glazed as she takes in the beautiful surroundings.

When we walk up the steps of the castle through the line of white wolves she stares in amazement. Finally, we reach the castle door and the old door man lets us into the castle. "Welcome back Samuel, I see you have a friend with you," and he smiles at Abs. Then he announces, "Unfortunately, the King and Queen are not able to see you today."

"That's okay Lupa, today we need to visit all the places where Princess Gazania used to spend her time. You can help us to look for clues and any unusual changes to the scene of the crime. If we meet anyone connected with the Princess...then we'd like to talk to them and add them to our suspect list."

"I think we should start with the Princess' bedroom," says Abs. That's where we will find out about her daily life. There will be lots of clues in her bedroom, maybe some secret letters or even a diary. Princesses always have diaries!" Lupa and I agree and so we set off into the castle to Princess Gazania's bedroom.

What a beautiful room she has. All decorated in

pink and white with flowers everywhere. It is obvious that Princess Gazania loves flowers.

She is named after a beautiful flower and her flower name means treasure. I am sure that is exactly what she is to her parents. Looking around the room, we see photos of her parents and pets and friends. All the typical things you would see in a twelve-year-old's bedroom...that belongs to a princess!

"We need to see if she had a diary," says Abs. "Let's look under her pillow and see if it is there."

Sure enough, there was the diary. Lupa and I looked very impressed. "How did you know that the Princess would have a diary under her pillow?" Lupa asked.

"Boys surely you know that every girl hides her diary under her pillow." She laughs, "Oops, I forgot, you two are not girls so how would you know that!"

We take the diary and put it in a bag as evidence.

"Where else did Princess Gazanis spend her time?" I ask Lupa.

"Our Princess loved the herb garden and she spent a lot of time there learning how to grow herbs and how to use them to help the animal kingdom."

"'Well let's go to the herb garden then. Please lead the way, Lupa."

Off we went, following Lupa, down a long passage in the castle. On the walls are pictures of the royal family, past Kings, and Queens. A row of family portraits. I stop and stare at some of them. Most of the Kings have kind faces and look handsome but one picture looks kind of mean and has very small and dark staring eyes. His eyes seem to look at you as you walk by. I shudder and have a quick look at the name under the portrait – Rumex, son of King Rhizome the second it says.

Rumex
Son of King Rhizome 2nd

The long passage comes to an end with a side door that leads out to the herb garden.

Abs shudders, "What a relief to be outside and away from the icy stare of Rumex!" And I totally agree!

The herb garden is behind the castle in a sheltered courtyard with a hedge all around it. Lupa takes us round to the gate leading into the herb garden. I feel a funny sort of shiver go down my spine as I realize this is what I was looking for when I first landed in Gardinia. Herbs, and how to grow them. There should be some powerful clues here I think.

The gate to the herb garden is impressive and as we

get close to it we hear some funny sounds. I whisper to Abs, "Can you hear that? It sounds like giggling." Abs nods her head, her eyes glance around us.

Someone is watching us and they seem to be amused. I wonder who they are. Lupa does not seem at all worried. He opens the gate and we walk into the herb garden.

We are greeted by a rush of little people all wanting to give us hugs! Every little person only comes up to our waists and they are dressed in very funny old-fashioned clothes. I smile and wave at Abs and try to ask who are these little people when Lupa comes to the rescue.

"Ahem, aaargh um," he clears his throat and gives everyone a chance to calm down.

"Allow me to introduce you all to...The Gnomes of Gazania's Herb Garden."

There is a general sound of laughter and chuckling about the introduction.

Lupa continues, "Gnomes are very modest and as you can see, sometimes they can be a little over-friendly!" They are passionate about gardening and keeping gardens in just the right way to make sure plants, animals and insects are living as they should. Alive and free."

Abs and I squeeze past Lupa into the herb garden. The gnomes are so excited to see us. We look at their garden and can see how great they are at gardening. All the plants are in neat rows. Little signs tell us what each herb is in the garden. At the end of the garden is a greenhouse and sign up that says 'Do Not Disturb'.

I am left wondering how so many gnomes came to be here in Gazania. I turn to ask Lupa and he tells me, "A few years before this day, the gnomes were released from their urban garden duties.

People all over the world felt that gnomes should not have to stay in gardens and so they were sent back to the forests and woodlands that they came from. This family of gnomes specially loved growing herbs and using them for medicinal purposes to help woodland animals.

When they were released from their country gardens they choose to come to Gardinia to help with growing herbs."

I saw Abs look sideways at Lupa but he nodded his head and said, "You can check for yourself, but it is true and we love having our gnomes. They are a real help with our gardens."

Lupa calls us over, "Samuel and Abs, this is our head gardener, Herbie." He is an old and wise gnome gardener with a very long beard. We feel very privileged to meet him.

"Welcome to Princess Gazania's herb garden and center for the protection of wounded and hurting animals," says Herbie. "We are her humble servants and are deeply stressed that our beautiful Princess is not here with us today."

I felt sorry for the gnomes, they all looked so sad. "Don't worry Herbie, we will find her. We will need your help to work out where the Princess is and who kidnapped her. Can we talk to the gnomes and find out if they have any clues to the disappearance of Princess Gazania."

The gnomes nod their heads and their little red hats bob up and down. The mutter among themselves and shake their heads.

Herbie explains, "The Princess was working with one of the most talented gnomes called Basil. He was in charge of the Greenhouse and the development of medicines and healing potions for the birds and animals in Gardinia."

Herbie signals us to follow him to the Greenhouse.

"The Princess and her gnome assistant, Basil were busy with top secret work," says Herbie.

"On the day that our Princess disappeared, her assistant, Basil, did not come to work either. Now all our experiments have had to stop. They were close to finding a special potion to help with night blindness in some of our nocturnal animals."

Abs and I go into the Greenhouse. We are followed by a crowd of eager gnomes but they stop at the door. They are not allowed into the secret lab where meds and potions are being made. Abigail is taking notes as we walk around. She is particularly interested in a plant has beautiful purple flowers on it and is labeled 'Deadly Night Shade'.

She nudges me to look at the plant but doesn't question the gnome. On her notepad she jotts: *Need to research this plant!* I nod and agree.

It's actually time for us to leave as we have to get back to the library before it closes. There is just time for one more question. I bend down and look into the gnome's eyes and ask, "Have you noticed anything else that is unusual?"

He nods his little head and tells us, "The bees seem

to have disappeared in the garden and we need them to pollinate the herbs. The bees have abandoned their hives and as summer is nearly at an end, there is not enough honey to feed the bees in winter."

This is very worrying news and I don't know what to say. Could this be connected to the disappearance of the Princess?

We thank the gnomes and explain we will be back again to investigate further. We leave with Lupa to walk down the path back to the library. It is always a bit scary walking along the path as the dark side of Gardinia stretches to the left of us. Every time I leave this land I feel the shadows growing larger. I am hoping the giant moths don't appear as I am sure Abs will be terrified.

I take a closer look at the spiky plants to the left of me. It looks as if they are covered in orange flowers.

I am just about to say something to Lupa about this curious crop when he says,"Our potato crop this year has been taken over by a plague of huge caterpillars. They have devoured all the leaves and left the plants unable to produce any fruit. They seem to have arrived from nowhere and within a few days have destroyed our crop that we need for winter food. The plants have totally changed, they no longer even look like potato plants."

I take a closer look at the creepy caterpillars!

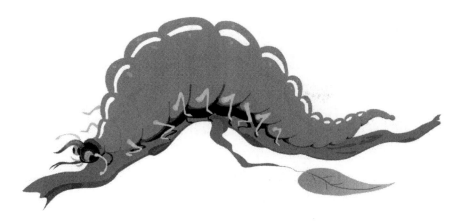

A shiver runs down my spine. I nudge Abs, "Look Abs, it is the same caterpillar as the one Miss Sorrel has in the library!" This is another clue to add to the crime scene.

Is Miss Sorrel connected to Gardinia and the missing Princess?

There is no time to speculate as the sun is setting. "Hurry Abs! We have to get back now." We wave farewell to Lupa and suddenly find ourselves sitting in a heap beneath the Botany shelf.

I motion to Abs to say I will call her. We leave in different ways and I rush home as fast as I can to put as much data on the crime scene board as I can.

Chapter 6 - Forensic Entomology at Work...

Abs and I dash out of the library. We are in a hurry to get home and review the information we gathered during our visit to Gardinia. I rush straight up to my bedroom to enter the clues I remember onto the storyboard. Abs has the Princess' diary and I am anxious to know if there is any vital information written on the pages of Gazania's personal diary.

I look at the storyboard. It is quite impressive. Everything has been written on note paper with sticky notes so the names and places can be moved around the board. Abs said this was important so we could connect clues together if they are related in any way. What is the connection between Miss Sorrel and the caterpillars? Why have the bees disappeared I wonder? I have had suspicions about Miss Sorrel from the beginning. Who is she really? And how did she come to be in our library - just when our librarian mysteriously disappeared? I put Miss Sorrel's name next to the big, bright caterpillar picture and shudder at the thought that they are connected.

The phone rings downstairs and Mom calls upstairs to say my friend Abigail is on the phone. I wonder what Abs wants. She must have found something interesting in the Princess' diary. Abs is quite breathless on the phone.

"We need to meet as soon as possible," she says in a loud whisper.

"What's the matter, Abs?" I ask with a tremble in my voice. "We can't meet till tomorrow and then it will have to be after school!"

Abs coughs politely over the phone so I know her Mom must be close by. She can't talk about what we are investigating. She just tells me in a chirpy voice that we need to get together to finish our project and could she come over tomorrow. I answer yes, but I wish I could know more of what she has discovered sooner.

It's time for dinner and Uncle Bert is joining us this evening. I wonder if there is a connection between the giant moths, brightly colored fierce caterpillars and disappearing bees. I group them together on the storyboard as they are all part of the insect world and I think if I get a chance I will slip a question to Uncle Bert. Maybe there is a link and it could have something to do with our case. Every bit of information is important...no matter how strange.

I find Uncle Bert in the lounge. He is just finishing off his tea and Mom is busy in the kitchen. I sit next to Uncle Bert and wait for the right moment to speak to him.

"Good evening Uncle Bert," I say politely. "Can I ask you an entomology question? Please?"

Uncle Bert is rather old-fashioned and loves to hear and see good manners. He nods and waits for the question.

"Well Uncle Bert, I was wondering if there is any connection between a brightly colored caterpillar, a giant moth, and bees?"

Uncle Bert thinks for a moment and then answers softly.

"Well actually, I don't want your mother to hear, but there is a connection between the Death's Head Hawk moth, brightly colored caterpillars, and honey which would also mean bees!"

I am fascinated and listen in awe as Uncle Bert explains that the Death's Head Hawk moth has a very brightly colored caterpillar as part of its life cycle. A sort of ugly but strangely beautiful caterpillar he tells me. When he describes the caterpillar he adds that it has very strong mandibles and a sharp horn sticking out. This caterpillar pupates underground and hatches into the Death's Head Hawk moth.

"Wow Uncle Bert, that is fascinating but what about the bees?" I ask. "They are not the same insect so how can they be connected to the moths?"

"Good question young Sam," says Uncle Bert.

He looks past my chair to see if my Mom is still in

the kitchen. When he sees she is still busy, he tells me more about the Death's Head Hawk moth. "This moth is a thief and lives a life of crime. It is very fond of honey. Death's Heads are masters of disguise and have a very thick skin so they don't get stung by the worker bees. They make a noise, a kind of squeaking that sounds like the Queen bee. This confuses the bees and allows the Death's Head Hawk moth to get into the hive and feast on the bees' precious honey. There have been pictures taken of hundreds of these moths feasting on the honey in the bees' hive."

I am absolutely amazed and keen to ask Uncle Bert more about his experience with these moths, but Mom bursts into the lounge and the conversation ends there and then.

"Supper's ready," she announces. Uncle Bert and I nod as we know this ends any other questions about Death's Head Hawk moths. I can't wait to eat supper and get upstairs to set this bit of information onto the storyboard. This could be a very important clue!

After supper, I rush upstairs into my room and close the door. Sitting at my desk I face the storyboard and add in my information from the latest visit to Gardinia. The first thing I do is to move all the insect related notes to the same spot. Miss Sorrel's gets placed next to them. I think there is more to her character in this story than I know.

Then I add in the gnomes that we met today. The little gnomes are surrounded by the herbs they grow and the picture looks quite sweet as they all wear their little red pointed hats and look very wise with their long beards. There is a picture of a greenhouse and the two important gnomes Herbert and Basil. Then I have added a castle picture and the King and Queen. I step back and wonder what else we will add to the story when Abs arrives.

Abs will add in the clues about the Princess and her diary. A few other pictures are on the side, as I don't know where to fit them in at this stage. There is the rest of the royal family, Uncle Ru, and this wife. We don't have a name for her. Finally a section for the dark side of Gardinia. Gray wolves, shadows and another castle hidden behind huge trees of some sort. I realize there is very little we know about the darker side of Gardinia. What part do the other wolves play in the garden world of Gardinia. I must be sure to ask Lupa why some wolves like himself are close to the royal family and why some live a different life lurking in the shadows.

Finally, I slip into bed and hope I can sleep. Tomorrow Abs and I will fill in more information on the storyboard and I will tell her how the insects have an impact on our investigation. Uncle Bert has helped me understand an interesting link between different groups of insects. Criminal moths and innocent bees – wow I never would have thought nature could be so fascinating and related to a life of crime.

Chapter 7 - The Princess' Diary...

I wake very early. I feel we are on the edge of a cliff and about to discover some very important evidence that will bring us closer to solving the disappearance of Gazania. I am sure her diary holds the key to some important clues into the reason why she disappeared without a trace. As soon as I get to school I look for Abs. She will be in my English class today but Abs is playing her role as an undercover cop very seriously. She ignores me completely and even when I try to give her a little wave she turns away as if she hasn't seen me. How annoying! I will have to wait for her to arrive at my house this afternoon with the diary. Then we can look at the diary notes and add clues to our storyboard. I hope she is going to be impressed with what I have found out and added to the investigation.

The school day seems to drag by and we don't have library lessons so I go home early. I have my own key to let myself in and I get ready for Abs to arrive. I tidy the room, get a cool drink and a few of my Mom's special homemade biscuits. These should be just the right goodies to keep us focused for the afternoon. Mom knows Abs is coming over to continue with our 'project'.

As soon as the doorbell rings I jump to my feet and run downstairs to let Abigail into the house. Her eyes are sparkling with anticipation and excitement.

I know she can't wait to share the contents of the diary with me. I am keen to show her the updated storyboard and the interesting facts I have learned about Death's Head Hawk moths - the criminals of the insect world.

"Oh Abs, I've discovered some very important information, I can't wait to fill you in!" I exclaimed, unable to contain my excitement.

Without wasting any time I tell Abs about the moths and the bees and the whole entomology story Uncle Bert told me about. "The insects and Mrs. Sorrel are grouped together! What their real link is we are not sure of yet. It's the diary I am anxious to hear about!" I say, talking so fast that the words blur together.

"I know you want to hear about Gazania's diary," says Abs slowly. "I have had a quick peep, but reading someone else's diary is actually not something we should do. It is a very personal part of a person."

I nod knowingly, but can't really see the significance of this, must be a girl thing!

Abs looks at me with a very serious face, "If we read the diary, you MUST promise that you will keep every word in confidence."

Abs is sure Gazania would approve as it will help the case, but a diary is a very private piece of property. She is clutching the diary to her chest, almost embracing it. I feel that if I don't agree I will never be able to learn what is in the Princess' diary and it could be the most important piece of evidence we have in our possession.

"Yes Abs, of course, I will not say a word about anything in the diary. I understand it is a very personal and sensitive possession that belongs to Princess Gazania. I am sure we will be able to return it to her soon," I reply. I hope that I sound sincere...when what I feel like saying is, *"Open up the diary and TELL ME WHAT IT SAYS!"*

Abs is satisfied and we sit together at the end of the bed to look at Princess Gazania's diary. It has an information page at the beginning and then a very interesting family tree that she has filled in.

Gazania has put her grandparent's names at the top of the family tree followed by her father King Costus Woodsonii and his younger brother Rumex Acetosa. They are the two sons of King Rhizome the Second. Then the family tree divides into Gazania's family, she is the only daughter of her father King Costus and her mother Queen Rosemary. Then on the other side of the family tree is Rumex (Uncle Ru) in brackets and his wife Bella Donna.

"Bella Donna is such a beautiful name, but it is so sad that she has no children," says Abs. Girls are so sensitive sometimes.

"That's the family tree," says Abs. "We have only met the King, well actually you met him. We have not met anyone else in the royal family."

I agree with Abs, that is true and this is the most important family of the land. "Abs, Lupa told me briefly about the family and the fact that Uncle Ru was jealous of his brother so Uncle Ru and his wife moved to another castle. Lupa didn't go into the nitty gritty, but I know they live in the castle on the dark-side of Gardinia. I've seen it from a distance, it is surrounded by tall trees and seems to be totally in a shadow." Even talking about the dark side left me feeling anxious and a little scared.

"Let's put these names on our storyboard," says Abs. "We can see if they fit in anywhere in our themes and if they provide clues to the disappearance of Gazania."

Both of us return to the diary and we both look carefully into what Gazania has written to see if there is anything that directly relates to the case. There are a lot of personal comments about loneliness and being an only child but the entries that catch our eyes are the ones about the herb garden and the gnomes.

Princess Gazania is very involved with the gnomes and in particular, the young gnome who is assisting her with her experiments. Together they are making healing potions for the woodland creatures. The gnome's name is Basil. She talks highly of him and praises him for his 'tireless work to help the small woodland animals.' The Princess goes every day to the animal hospital and to the laboratory to see how the different medicines are coming along. She makes sure every experiment is recorded and that the right animals get treated. Basil is beside her all the way and has a natural ability to choose the right herbs to combine for the right medicine.

Every day the Princess has an entry in her diary that is filled with encouragement for the new center. She is excited because it is going to help so many creatures. Her entries in the diary are full of joy and she is clearly thrilled with the work Basil is doing.

Then suddenly the tone of the diary entries changes. There is interference from her aunt Bella Donna and Gazania's last entry says...

'I need to put a stop to Bella Donna's visits to the greenhouse. I fear her intentions are not honorable. She is trying spy on our work and take ideas from our new experiments.'

The Princess continues...

'Bella Donna is a forceful woman and I worry about the way she looks at poor Basil. He is afraid of her and when she visits he tries to hide under the nearest plant pot. His hiding space is always a giveaway as his shivering makes the pot rattle.'

The entry for that day ends with...

'Uncle Ru and Bella Donna have set themselves apart from the family. They have their own castle and I know my father suspects they have changed and are involved in some dark and suspicious activities. The gray wolves have become their servants and the shadows over their part of Gardinia do not encourage the growth of healthy happy plants.'

Finally, Gazania says...

'I am afraid and must speak to my father about more protection for me and the gnomes of the herb garden. Perhaps he will consider a permanent white wolf guard at the gate.'

"That's the last entry," says Abs. We both look at each other and then slowly go to the storyboard to add the new names and any comments.

I put all the Gardinia people in one place. Together we look carefully at their names and who they are.

Suddenly, I have a brainwave!

"Abs, what if there is a theme amongst the people from Gardinia, like the insects are linked in a way. Maybe the people have a link that could help us understand more about Gardinia."

Abs and I continue to stare at the storyboard and suddenly Abs says with a gasp, "Everyone in Gardinia is named after a plant. The gnomes are all named after herbs, Gazania is a flower, and her mother is a flowering herb. The original King was called Rhizome, a kind of root. I think if we research all their names we may find there is some hidden clue we have missed."

Abs points to the storyboard. "Let's take their names and see if we can find a connection."

I agree with her, it is worth a try. We have two new names to add. Uncle Rumex and his wife Bella Donna.

They must be key figures in this mystery. What do their names mean and how do they fit into the plant world? "Abs, I think we will have to visit the library tomorrow," I say.

"Look what I happen to have!" says Abs with such a smirk on her face.

She pulls a gigantic Botany book out of her bag. '1001 Plants and Their Names' is the title.

"You are so clever Abigail! Let's look at the suspect's names and see if we can find a link to the crime committed in Gardinia a week ago."

Abs pulls out this thick book, "Let's start with B she says, Bella Donna," she says. I am ready to write up information for the storyboard.

"Bella Donna," Abs reads with a gasp, "is another name for the deadly poisonous plant called The

Deadly Night Shade."

Surely there is a connection between Bella Donna and the purple flower that was in the greenhouse. I see Abs is keen to continue so I keep that thought on hold and listen to the research of the next name.

Abs continues, "King Costus Woodsonii is the name of a ginger plant and the ginger plant grows from a tuber or rhizome."

That makes him the son of King Rhizome the Second. That is an easy one and nothing sinister there.

"The gnomes are all named after herbs and I don't think they are capable of anything wicked. What is the last name on the storyboard?"

"Uncle Ru, Rumex Acetosa is his full name," Abs says out loud as she searches through the book. She goes through the book alphabetically until she reaches R for Rumex. I see her freeze and she turns pale. She is in a state of shock.

"Oh Sam, you are not going to believe this! Rumex is the botanical name for Sorrel!"

I look at Abs and am speechless, she breaks the
silence by saying," Do you think Miss Sorrel and
Uncle Ru are the same people?"

"Yes Abs, I do. I am sure of it. This can't be a
coincidence."

"Even though Uncle Ru is a man and Miss Sorrel is
a woman?" asks Abs with a tremble in her voice.

I nod my head and try to put my thoughts together.
"Let's face it Abs, she's weird! She has a hairy chin,
a big Adam's apple, and a very deep voice. She
doesn't really like children. She calls me SPROG

making fun of my name! And she has more time for a rather ugly caterpillar than the children in the library. Oh and what about that weird tattoo on the back of her neck?"

"Abs, I think that Uncle Ru and Miss Sorrel are one and the same person and Uncle Ru is up to NO good. I think he is a magician and with his magical powers, he has deceived us into thinking he is a woman. He is a master of disguises. Actually, a bit like the Death's Head Hawk moth. He has entered our world and tricked us into thinking he is a female librarian."

Abigail and I stare at each other as this piece of evidence sinks in. What are we going to do now?

I tell Abs, "We should keep this very quiet while we carry on with our investigation and get more pieces of the puzzle put together. I am sure Uncle Bert will agree that we cannot blow our cover before we know where Princess Gazania is."

"Sam," says Abs in a very serious voice. "We need to go back to Gardinia and speak to the gnomes. They were Gazania's closest friends and I think it is possible that one of the gnomes may be too afraid to speak up."

I nod my head in agreement. We will have to plan our next visit to Gardinia soon. We have to make some smart moves if we are going to outwit Uncle Ru or Miss Sorrel whatever we decide to call him/her.

"We must arrange a meeting with the gnomes before anyone else is in danger!"

Abigail nods her head in agreement and we decide that tomorrow afternoon during library study time, we will prepare to go back to Gardinia. Abs gets up to leave with the Princess diary under her arm. She's very possessive of the diary, our best evidence so far. I want to tell her it should stay here with the storyboard. However, I see she has pulled the diary in close to her heart and so I let her take it away with her. She will probably put it under *her* pillow. It's a girl thing - I remind myself, as I show Abs out and say goodbye.

Chapter 8 - Chervil the courageous little gnome...

I am a little nervous to go to the library the next day. What if Miss Sorrel realizes that Abs and I know who she or he is? I don't want to make things any more complicated than they are. Miss Sorrel might be suspicious that we know who she really is. We have learned that there is a dark side to Gardinia. And who is Miss Sorrel, is she Uncle Ru, is Miss Sorrel/Uncle Ru the mastermind behind some clever plot. I am not even sure if I understand the extent of the plan to upset the King and Queen of Gardinia. We have got to stop Uncle Ru before he succeeds in bringing Gardinia down and over-throwing King Costus, his brother.

I meet Abs at the library door. We know the drill now. Don't greet each other, collect our browser sticks and walk swiftly to the Botany section. We double check we have our 3D glasses. I am all ready to sneak past the librarian's counter when a deep voice calls out, "Hmmm, its Sprog. In a bit of a hurry are you boy?" she asks with a sneer on her face.

I freeze on the spot and cannot think of anything to say.

"You know the rules," says Miss Sorrel. "No running in the library! I will have to demerit your readathon points."

Then she adds something ridiculous that sounds

like a throaty rumble. I realize she is laughing as she points out that I am still on Zero!

I am furious but have to control my temper. I just slip away while she is still chuckling to herself.

I promise myself there and then that I will have the last laugh.

Thank goodness I find Abs around the next corner. She looks nervous and excited at the same time. I signal her to put on her 3D glasses and hold her hand and together we make our way back into Gardinia to visit the gnomes in Gazania's herb garden.

We greet Lupa as we arrive. "Hi Lupa," I say, "today we need to visit the gnomes. Abs and I think that one of the gnomes may know something and be too scared to share." Lupa nods his head and heads off towards along the path to the garden.

Going into the herb garden is amazing! Everything smells wonderful and the gnomes keep it so neat and tidy. The smell of fresh herbs is all around us. I feel sure we will find some more clues. This was a special place in Princess Gazania's life. The herb garden gates swing open and we are surrounded by little people all trying to get into the act of being helpful.

Suddenly Lupa gives out a howl and everyone comes to a halt. "Our friends have come to help us find the Princess and Basil. We need any clues that you may have. It is your duty to step forward and tell us anything that may help."

There is a bit of low mumbling amongst the gnomes but no one seems eager to step forward and volunteer information. Finally, Lupa says, "You won't get into trouble, we really need your help to find our beautiful Princess. So if you know anything, please I beg of you, please step forward."

There is a hushed silence and suddenly in one huge movement of gnome figures...all the gnomes step back and one little gnome is left at the front of the crowd standing on his own.

It's little Chervil, Basil's assistant. He is trembling from head to toe and looking pale. His little-pointed hat is shaking like a leaf and his teeth are chattering.

Lupa looks down at the gnome and says,"So little one, do you know something about the disappearance of these two special people?"

"If you do," he continues. "You need to come with us and tell us everything you know."

Chervil obeys Lupa and together we all walk to the greenhouse to hear what Chervil has to say.

I can see he is scared and I want to be sympathetic but if our questioning is to be successful we must help him understand that this is an investigation and every bit of information no matter how small counts.

"So master Chervil, "I begin. "What can you tell us about the night that Princess Gazania and Basil disappeared?" I think that sounds quite official and Abigail has her notebook ready.

Chervil pours out his story as we listen and try to take it all in. "That night," he says, "the Princess, Basil and himself were close to finishing our tests on the 'night blindness potion'. The Princess was just holding the bottle up to the light to check on the color and clarity of the medicine when there was a loud sound like thunder and the doors burst open. I had a chance to hide, but the other two were left standing in front of a tall woman in a purple dress. Two gray wolves came with her. The tall lady pulled a small bag out from under her skirt, opened it and blew some black dust over the Princess and

Basil. Immediately the two of them fell asleep."

Chervil was crying, "I watched the tall woman put Gazania and Basil on the wolves backs. Then they disappeared into the dark night."

"I was so scared," he said. "I could not move until the next morning. When I did move there was so much going on about the mysterious disappearance that I was not able to share what I knew. I am sorry I did not help you sooner."

Abs and I reassure the little gnome. "It's okay Chervil, we know how scared you are. Thank you for telling us about the lady in purple, you have been a big help."

The little gnome bows and runs off as quickly as he can.

It is time for Abs, Lupa and I to discuss this evidence and what we are going to do with the knowledge that Princess Gazania and her scientist gnome Basil have been kidnapped. Lupa tells us that the only person who would be dressed in a purple dress and have the ability to kidnap two people at once would be Bella Donna herself.

This is definitely a big piece of the puzzle. Maybe Lupa can add some interesting information to the story.

"Lupa, why did you look so sad at the mention of the gray wolves?" I asked.

Lupa tells me that once all the wolves were together in the protection of Gardinia. Sadly when Uncle Ru and Bella Donna moved to their own castle they told the gray wolves that they would be better off living in the gray shadows of the dark side and so the gray wolves parted company from the white wolves believing they would be better off on the dark side of Gardinia.

Worry lines creased around Lupa's eyes. "The wolf pack was very sad to see them go. We feel they may be under some sort of spell that keeps them trapped in the dark shadows with Bella Donna as their mistress."

We are just about to leave the greenhouse when I notice the unusual plant with the purple flowers has also disappeared. The deadly night shade plant has been stolen and the notes made by the Princess.

Lupa, Abs and I gather outside the Greenhouse and sit quietly thinking about everything.

I announce, "We need a plan of action. I think we all know what the next step will have to be...but it will take a lot of planning and courage from all of us." We nod silently in agreement and it's Abs who speaks up.

"Friends," she says with a very serious voice. "We will have to visit the dark-side of Gazania and try to get into the castle, the home of Uncle Ru and Bella Donna."

Lupa and I nod our heads. We know this is the solution but how, when and with whom.

Lupa looks very serious.

He tells us that the dark-side of Gardinia has become its own land and getting in there is impossible. The trees and bushes are overgrown and all-round the castle are these tall stinging trees. Lupa thinks they are called Gympie trees. They are not the kind of trees that King Costus and Queen Rosemary would want to grow. They are vicious and their sting is very painful, even deadly. It seems like an impossible situation.

"Let us take our problem to the Gnome Council," Lupa says thoughtfully. "They are very wise and have inside knowledge into how to solve problems using our natural resources."

We all nod in agreement and walk off with determination to meet the Gnome Council.

The Gnome Council is made up of the five wisest and oldest gnomes. They all have very long beards and big pointed hats. They sit in a row in front of us. Lupa has already explained our situation. The Gnome Council stroke their beards and make 'thinking noises'. They confer with one another and finally, the oldest gnome with the longest beard stands up to speak.

We all listen in awe and wait for his pearls of wisdom.

"I would like to thank you all sincerely for your concern for beloved Princess and our very talented gnome Basil. We, the Gnome Council would like to help in every way that we can to stop the wicked Bella Donna and Rumex and their evil plans. Your plan to go to the castle on the dark-side is very noble. It is dangerous and unfriendly there," says the senior gnome of the council.

Abs and I look at the council with wide eyes but we want to hear what they have to say.

"We think that you should use our woodland animals to help you as they know the forests and woodland paths. However, as the route to the dark castle is full of dangerous plants we think you should consider flying over the forest and getting to the castle from the top. We would like to suggest that if you are keen we can talk to the Giant Eagle Owl and see if he will fly you over the forest and into the dark-side of Gardina." The chief gnome looks carefully at us, his eyes stressing how serious the situation was.

Abigail and I nod earnestly. We know the dangers but have committed to helping the people of Gardinia. If this is the way to do it then we are going to try. We agree that the gnomes can arrange the flight and we are about to leave when another gnome speaks up.

And he adds, "We would like to offer a backup plan through our gnome tunnel that goes underground and may be used as an escape for you when you have managed to get into the dark castle."

This is an amazing offer as the gnomes don't usually share their tunnel information. They have tunnels that lead to their treasure and are well known for tunneling. A backup plan will be an amazing reassurance for us.

Abs and I know it is time to leave as we have to get out of the library before it closes. We tell Lupa that we will have to make a plan to get back...but it will have to be in the dark of night. We cannot say when or how we will do this. Lupa assures us that he will have everything on standby and we will just need to be ready for a night flight on a Giant Eagle Owl.

Wow, how amazing will that be! Abs and I walk down the path to leave Gardinia. I feel so sad as I look to the left and see the fields of potatoes completely destroyed. The plants have no leaves, just spikes. The caterpillars are gone and it is clear there will be no potato crop this year.

 Abs and I leave as we always do and make our way out of the library. As we pass the librarian's desk we notice that the caterpillar in Mrs. Sorrel's jar has also disappeared. The jar is left with dry leaves and some sand at the bottom. What has happened to the brightly colored caterpillar?

Chapter 9 - When a plan comes together...

I am home and in a terrible state. I have new clues to enter on the storyboard and new plans and a strategy to think about. The gnomes have been amazing and have offered so much to support our investigation. Gnomes never share information leading to their tunnels because they usually have treasure buried there. The Gnome Council has given us their word that we will have a backup plan and can use their secret tunnel that goes under the dark side of Gardinia.

I put all the new information onto the storyboard and begin to think about how we can get to the dark-side of Gardinia soon. Now we know who the enemy really is and what has happened to Princess Gazania and Basil we have a duty to go to their rescue. I feel I need to try and get some more under-cover advice from Uncle Bert. He is coming to supper again tonight and so maybe a carefully aimed question will prompt some useful information into crime scene investigation.

I hear Uncle Bert knock on the door and so I let him in, get him some tea and Mom's biscuits. When he is settled I sit next to him ready to ask a few questions.

"Hi Uncle Bert," I say. "Have you had a nice day?"

Uncle Bert nods and concentrates on his tea and biscuits. I wait for the right moment to ask him a question that I will pretend is part of my school project.

"Erhem," I clear my throat to get Uncle Bert's attention. He looks up from his tea and nods to show he is listening. Then he puts his cup down and I can see he is ready to answer my questions.

"I was wondering, Uncle Bert, did you ever organize a search and rescue mission?"

Uncle Bert looked thoughtful for a moment and then replied, "Yes, young Sam, there were many of those operations during my time as a forensic entomologist. Some very interesting ones, but I think the most daring missions were the ones that we organized at night."

I hold my breath at this point because this is just the way I want the conversation to go. Search and rescue at night will be the way forward to rescue Princess Gazania and gnome Basil. I feel a mixture of excitement and fear come over me. A visit to the dark-side of Gardinia is going to be a necessary part of our plan. We will only have one opportunity...so it will have to be very well organized.

"It is very important to be well organized and know your enemy," says Uncle Bert in a serious voice.

"You need to be prepared for any eventuality. A night rescue is far more dangerous because your enemy has more opportunity to find hiding places."

Uncle Bert adds with a very serious tone in his voice. "Camouflage is a key part of any rescue and at night you have to be invisible. Like a cat burglar. A black cat burglar."

Uncle Bert pauses for a moment before adding instructions about clothing, communications and the pre-ops room to map out the rescue. A firm briefing for everyone he says. But most important of all – know your enemy because they probably already know you!

I have one last question and am sure Uncle Bert can answer this one because of his knowledge of insects. There is definitely a link between the hawk moths, Uncle Ru and the plans to overthrow King Costus. My question gets a raised eyebrow from Uncle Bert and I know he is intrigued.

"Uncle Bert, if you are investigating a case with a strong presence of an insect, like a moth?" I ask and I try to choose my words with care. "How closely do you think the villain will follow the insect's life cycle?"

"In my experience Sam, the villain is usually obsessed with the insect behavior." Uncle Bert lowers his voice and continues, "You have to be very careful with the villain who associates with a moth like the Death's Head because the skull on the back of the moth has, through the course of history, been part of dark and magical mysteries – even witchcraft!"

Uncle Bert adds some interesting facts about these moths. I nod my head as I know now that part of the plan Uncle Ru has is linked to the moth's pupa stage of its life cycle. We will need to act quickly to get into the dungeons of the dark castle before the moths hatch.

I thank Uncle Bert and can see him looking sideways at me as I head upstairs to rearrange the storyboard. The caterpillars are scratched out and the pupa stage of the moth's cycle is added in. The caterpillars on the dark-side of Gardinia are busy developing into moths and the caterpillar in the library is in that phase too. Abs and I have to get into action. It's time to call Abs and tell her what Uncle Bert has said, then see what we can do to get a search and rescue plan together.

"Abs, it's urgent we meet after school, we need to set up a search and rescue mission and we need to do it quickly," I say, sounding very serious. We agree to meet during the chess club break as everyone knows we play chess together and that will not alert any comments from anyone.

Sure enough, we manage to meet between chess games and I tell Abs the latest news and comments from Uncle Bert.

We go through all the different options and the players in this next phase of our investigation. The big problem we have right now is how to get into Gazania under cover and in the middle of the night. It is going to be a very dangerous mission as we know nothing about the dark-side of Gazania. We have to be able to leave the library during the night and not be noticed to be able to see what is going on. Managing to do this during the day has been one thing, but during the night is just a lot more demanding.

Suddenly Abs face lights up like a firework display. "I've got an idea!" she says. "Tomorrow is the quiz night and the annual school camp out on the main field. It's the perfect opportunity to sneak back into the library and go to Gardinia during the night!"

I can see Abigail is super excited about this idea. I nod my head in agreement, but I don't think she is going to like what I have to say about the finer details of the plan.

"It's a great opportunity to find a way to get through the library Abs, well done. The problem I have with the idea is that I think only one of us should go into the dark-side castle and I think that I will have to take that responsibility. Sorry Abs," I add with great sincerity.

I see Abs' face drop and she is clearly disappointed but she is a good sport and great partner. She agrees it's best.

"I will you to cover for me if anything goes wrong

and it will be easier for one person to find their way into the castle and most important of all, find their way out again with Princess Gazania and her gnome assistant," I explain, feeling slightly guilty for leaving her out of the adventure.

My plan is to come to the quiz night dressed in dark clothes and all the things I think I need for the search and rescue mission. I know the gnomes will be ready on the other side in Gardinia. Abs is going to cover for me after the quiz and I am going to hide in the library and when everyone has gone to the campout, I will go to Gardinia.

Abs will cover for me at the campout. "Don't worry Sam, if anyone asks where you are I'll tell them that you aren't feeling well," says Abs.

I just need a few hours to get into the dark castle and out again. Then the gnomes and Lupa can return Gazania to her parents and Basil to his gnome family.

It all seems quite simple. Maybe too simple! I'm a bit nervous and leave the library with my hat pulled firmly over my eyes. Miss Sorrel has her head buried under the library counter. She is shuffling papers and library cards but I have bigger things to think about and am grateful to be able to leave unnoticed.

Chapter 10 - The Dark-Side of Gardina...

Everyone at school is excited and buzzing with talk about the quiz and the camp out on the field. Abs and I are excited too, but our feelings have nothing to do with the school activities. I have brought my old black ski pants and a black hat for my night camo outfit. I also have a long sleeve black pull over and black socks and trainers. I had to paint over the white stripe down the side so that I am completely covered in black. I have a few items in an old black kit bag but am not sure if I will take these into the castle.

The plan is to take part in the quiz so everyone sees me at school. Then in the confusion of everyone leaving to go to the field and meet their teachers, I will slip behind one of the library shelves and wait for the library to close. Abs reminds me to have a browser stick at hand for the rite of passage into Gardinia. When I think the coast is clear I will go to the Botany shelf and disappear. Those few moments in the library will be scary but luckily there is a full moon tonight so there will be some light to see by.

Abigail is ready with a story to tell anyone who asks where I am, but she thinks everyone will be so busy and excited about the camping part of the evening that no one will even notice I am not there.

"Sam, I'm a bit worried about the bees and the stinging Gympie trees," she says with a hint of fear in her eyes. She has brought along some seriously strong gardening gloves and some funny looking gauze to put over my head. "You may need these as protection," she says.

I laugh at the thought of a net over my head. When I see Abs is a bit hurt by my response, I assure her, "Thanks, heaps Abs, I promise I'll use them if I need them, you are such a great friend."

The quiz goes by in a blur of questions and answers. The children rush out of the library heading towards the campout. I hang back and take a side step into the Botany section of the reference books. I catch a last glimpse of Abs as she sneaks a little wave and then I hear the sliding doors close. I am alone in the library! When I am sure that I really am alone, I change into my cat burglar camo- outfit and prepare to be swept up into Gardinia.

I land with a bump right at the foot of the castle path and watch and wait for Lupa to meet me. It is evening and the light is fading.

Lupa arrives and I follow him to the gnome's garden cottages.

He knocks on the first cottage door and the chief of the Gnome Council appears. He nods his head and leads us to the back of his cottage. Everything is ready for our search and rescue mission. A map of the gnome tunnels, a headlight for me to wear and a snack pack of special gnome homely treats prepared by his wife. All that's missing is the giant eagle owl to carry me into the dark-side of Gardinia. At that moments there is a scuffling sound and a little gnome, also all dressed in black is standing beside me. He has replaced his pointed gnome hat with a black beanie and looks like a mini me. It is Chervil.

I try not to look surprised as he says, "I am reporting for duty to assist you in the search and rescue operation. I want to volunteer to help the Princess Gazania and her scientist, Basil, to escape."

I am about to tell Chervil that he is far too small and that I think he should stay at home with his family. However, I can see he is not going to leave and actually in gnome years he is probably not that young. I nod my head and agree.

"Welcome aboard Chervil, you are a very brave little gnome," I say sincerely.

At that precise moment, there is a swooshing sound of enormous wings and the giant eagle owl swoops into the back yard and settles down in front of us. He bows really low and flutters his giant eagle owl eyes showing off the most amazing orange eyes.

I wish I had more time to admire this magnificent bird and his enormous strong legs and beak but we have a mission to accomplish and must get going. We need the cover of the dark night. The owl has a large basket that he is going to use to carry us across the overgrown forest and past the dangerous stinging Gympie trees. He will drop us off inside the castle grounds as close to the dungeon entrance as possible. Little Chervil hops in the basket first and then I join him.

"Basil, the gnome, is my best friend," Chervil explains. "We grew up together. I must help him to escape, even if it is dangerous. Thank you for letting me come along Sam."

"I agree, Chervil, best friends should always stick together," and I think for a moment of Abs and how she has helped me since I started to be involved in trying to rescue Princess Gazania.

Together we hang onto the side of the basket as the giant eagle owl lifts us up into the air. The basket sways a bit and I feel just a tiny wave of air sickness come over me. It soon passes as we look over the edge of the basket into the dark forest and huge bushes that cover this side of Gardinia. I have no idea of what may be lurking in the forest below and just looking at it makes goose bumps appear on my arms.

Suddenly the towers and spires of the dark castle loom into sight. I wonder if this castle has a name. What would Bella Donna and Uncle Ru call their home?

As we get closer the eagle dips down towards the castle gates. They are dark and black and covered with a thick creeper. At the top of the gates, you can just make out the name, Chillingsgate Castle. The dark-side castle does have a name and it sends shivers down my spine.

The giant eagle owl flies steadily over the gates towards the first set of towers at the top of the castle. We are going to get off here and make our way down into the castle and go right down into the depths of the castle's dungeon and hope that this is where Bella Donna and Uncle Rumex are putting their plans together.

Under the cover of night with the moon and some stars, we make our way through the castle's gate and find the entry that leads down to the castle's dungeons.

Some light is provided by a fire torch. The shadows from these flames cast weird shapes all around us.

We creep down the spiral stairway and hope we will soon reach the dungeon. Finally, we are rewarded by finding a large room at the bottom of the stairs. In the middle of this room is an enormous table and it is laid out as if it is a game of model figures waiting to go into battle. I have seen similar games in model toy shops but this one is different. As I get closer I realize that this isn't just any game board. This board has some very interesting figures placed on it! There is a white castle with white wolves around it and a King and Queen sitting on their thrones. There is a path leading up the center of the board and on one side of the path, there is a little village of cottages and a greenhouse with a herb garden.

I get closer to the board and see a cluster of gnomes standing outside the village and then with a shudder I realize the game board is Gardinia. The one side of the board is the kingdom of King Costus and the gnomes are there in his kingdom.

The other side of the board is dark and gray. Its castle looks gloomy and foreboding. The dark castle, Chillingsgate castle, is protected by the gray wolves and I see each wolf is standing on a storybook. What an interesting platform for the wolves, a connection to the library perhaps. It looks as if one of the wolves is missing as there is a book on the board without a wolf figurine.

I look at Chervil and whisper, "What is Uncle Ru's game plan?"

Chervil looks terrified, he shakes his head and I can see that his knees are knocking together.

I walk a bit closer to get a look at the gnomes and the greenhouse and then draw back in shock! There are two extra figures with the gnomes, two taller figures in Bedford View uniforms, a boy and a girl. A big shiver goes down my spine as I realize it is me and Abs!

We thought we were super undercover cops and that no one knew we were involved. How wrong we are! What did Uncle Bert say? Know your enemy. Oh my, how silly we have been to think that Miss Sorrel or Uncle Ru was not aware of who we are.

Suddenly I realize I am in great danger. All the mean talk in the library and deliberate interference with my readathon points are part of their wicked plans. I wonder why the library is part of the plan to destroy Gardinia. I decide to keep that thought for another time. Right now we need to get as close as we can to the kidnapped Princess and the little gnome who was captured with her.

Chervil and I study the game board. "Samuel," whispers the gnome, "I think they plan to overthrow King Costus!"

I must not forget the storyboard that Abs and I have created. We had some pretty smart ideas and clues to lead us to the point of knowing Uncle Ru was behind the kidnapping. If Uncle Ru is playing war games then what is his secret weapon. Kidnapping Gazania is only a part of this evil plan to take over Gardinia. Uncle Ru has something else up his wicked sleeve.

I am trying to figure this out when I feel someone tugging at my top. It's Chervil. He beckons me to follow him and we go cautiously across the room to a large wooden door that is bolted from the outside.

Behind the door, we hear the sound of someone calling in a hoarse whisper, "Help me!"

Chervil and I listen carefully and try to open the door. My helpful little gnome pulls a pin from his pocket and picks the lock. Then we pull back the huge bolts that keep it locked. It is tough but we manage. In this deep, dark room sitting all alone is Basil. He stumbles out of the room and we wait for Gazania to follow. There is no sign of the Princess!

Basil shakes his head and wipes a tear from under his eye.

"She is not here," he says sadly. "They have taken her somewhere else and there was nothing I could do to save her."

I can tell he is devastated and Chervil tries to comfort his friend. What are we going to do now? Gazania is not here?

Basil takes a deep breath and stands tall. "We cannot go back to the King without his precious treasure, his daughter Gazania. I refuse to leave her in this dark and dangerous place."

All three of us walk over to the games board again. "Maybe there is something we have missed," I say, encouraging the gnomes to take a closer look.

"Look there is a passage and it is leading to an underground cave," cries Chervil excitedly.

"I want you two to wait here while I take a look at the cave." The gnomes agree.

I am not prepared in any way for what I see!

The cave is full of bees!

This is where all of Gardinia's bees are right now, but the astonishing thing is they are sharing this cave with their enemy, the Death's Head Hawk moth. The big brown moths are feeding side by side with the bees on the honey they have made. The honey that has been stolen to feed the moths and make them big and strong. Could this be Uncle Ru's secret weapon? A garden without bees cannot flourish as the bees must pollinate the flowers and bees need their honey to survive the winter when they hibernate and wait for the spring to start their cycle all over again.

The giant moths are very scary and an army of moths will cause a lot of damage to the gardens of Gardinia as they lay eggs and their caterpillars hatch out into munching monsters. It will be like a great plague!

Gently, so as not to disturb the bees and the gigantic moths, I close the door to the cave and go back to Uncle Ru's massive operations room. Basil and Chervil are waiting there.

"I think we should leave this place now!" I say. "The Princess is not here and if we are discovered in this room who knows what will become of us."

Uncle Bert's words are echoing in my ear – 'know your enemy'. While I am here in the depths of Uncle Ru's castle...I must take a few mental notes before I leave. There is clearly a mastermind behind this whole plan and looking at the game board I feel there is not much time before the final battle is going to take place. Uncle Ru has already placed his little figurine behind King Costus' throne ready to take over. The Princess, next in line to the throne has disappeared. The army of moths is ready and waiting but something is missing.

I look round the room and then I see the glass jar with the deadly night shade plant. The missing figure is Bella Donna. Basil steps forward as he sees me looking at the plant.

Basil says in a very hushed whisper, "Bella Donna is very clever and she knows a lot about plants and herbal remedies. Some plants can be used for good and evil. If the deadly nightshade gets into the wrong hands its leaves can be used to make a deadly poison. But in the right hands, it can be used to heal and help."

While I try to take this information in...Basil whispers something to Chervil. Chervil shakes his head and looks very worried. When I ask what is wrong, Chervil tells me Basil wants to stay behind and insists that we leave right now before it is too late.

I am shaking my head but Basil says firmly, "If I go with you then Uncle Ru will send the gray wolves to chase after us. You will not outrun the wolves and it will force Rumex to go ahead with his plan earlier. I will stay and be able to see what is going on inside the castle. I am learning a lot from Bella Donna and she is learning from me. Perhaps I can use some gnome wisdom to help her see how powerful medicine can be used to do good in our land."

Basil hands me a jar and inside it are some very angry bees. I wonder what this is all about when I see that one of the bees is much bigger than the others. It is the Queen bee.

In a quiet but demanding voice, Basil says, "You and Chervil should return to the gnome village with the Queen bee so she can start another colony. Don't worry about me, I will be safe. Bella Donna won't harm me, she needs me to teach her about the plants. And the Princess is not here so you should leave and use the new clues to work out where she has been taken."

Basil is right. I nod in agreement. He will stay and we must go back to plan for the next part of the rescue. Where is Gazania? I know our time is up, it will be morning soon.

We all get a fright as we hear steps coming down the path that led to the cave. Someone is coming in from the outside.

What a relief, it is a garden gnome. He is all dressed in his tunneling clothes with a little miner's lamp on his head. He beckons to us to follow him. I put on my gloves to protect my hands and pull my hat down over my ears. No one will see how ridiculous I look in the tunnel.

"Hurry up," says Basil, "someone is coming down the stairs; lock me back in my room. Don't worry about me and in this way, no one will know you have been here."

Basil goes back to his dungeon cell and I follow the gnomes into their tunnel clutching the jar of bees and hoping we will get back to the gnome village without any trouble. That will not be the end of my journey as I still have to get into the library and home again without being noticed.

Chapter 11 - Finding Gazania...

I land back in the library with the usual bump. This time arriving in the early hours of the morning. I rub my eyes in case the evening before was a dream. Looking down I see I am still in my cat burglar camo-kit and am clutching a black bag. There is something in the bag, I rustle my hands around and bring out a neat little parcel wrapped in cabbage leaves. It is the gnome treats from the night before. My journey to the dark-side was 'for real' and now I am back in the library. Quickly I change into my normal clothes and stuff my camo kit into the black bag. It's time to unwrap the gnome treat and munch on some delicious gnome gingerbread. This will have to be my breakfast today. Just as I am about to tiptoe into the library the doors open and the happy campers burst in chattering and yawning and telling tales from the night before.

Next thing Abs is by my side. I nod to say I am okay. "We need to meet and add to the storyboard," I tell her in a hushed whisper.

Abs gives thumbs up to agree and asks quietly, "Where is Gazania?"

I see the look of shock in her eyes when I shake my head and look away before anyone wonders why we are whispering in the library.

One of the teachers from the camp-out tells everyone that school is closing early so everyone can go home and catch up on their sleep. Abs and I exchange glances and I show her three fingers to indicate three o-clock this afternoon is when we will meet. Abigail, always good at sign language, nods back.

I am just about to leave the library when I notice Miss Sorrel is not in yet. The library counter is unattended. This would be a great opportunity to slip behind the counter and see if there are any clues to help us find Gazania. Uncle Ru has hidden the Princess somewhere. Maybe in his other disguise, as Miss Sorrel, he has left some evidence of where the Princess may be.

There are boxes and papers all stacked behind the library counter. Each class has a box with their lending cards in it. I scratch around and see the one belonging to my class. At the end of the box is an extra library pocket and in it are all my reading tokens that should be up on the readathon chart. I am furious with Miss Sorrel, how mean to hide my tokens in the back of the library card box. I shake my head in disbelief, but then realize who I am really dealing with, Miss Sorrel AKA Uncle Rumex. Abs thinks this is how we should address his character on the storyboard. AKA is an abbreviation for 'also known as' Abs tells me this so we will not get confused as to who Miss Sorrel is.

This is also part of the 'know your enemy' advice from Uncle Bert. Our enemy is a master of disguises and a magician too. I do think however, he makes a very untidy librarian. There is another box of library cards right at the back of the shelf. They don't have the normal names on the front but have little emblems of gray wolves. One of them has the number 398.2 in front of the pocket. Inside the pocket is a card with a little crown and a date.

I write all this down quickly to share with Abs and leave the cards at the back of the library counter. Hopefully, Miss Sorrel AKA Uncle Ru will not notice anything has been touched as it is already untidy. I'm exhausted and need to go home and sleep before Abigail arrives at three o-clock. A rushed exit from the library will get me home quickly.

When the doorbell rings at three I have updated the storyboard with all the new information. The war games board is now the center point with all the figures indicated. I know Abs will get a shock when she sees we are there with the gnomes. Standing on their books, in a symbolic circle, are the wolves. At the side of the board is the passage to the cave of bees. In the cave, the bees that have been deceived by the Death's Head Hawk moths and are sipping the honey from the honeycomb. I draw a picture of the Queen bee in a jar so I remember to tell Abs the Queen bee is safe and back with the gnomes. We did save some royalty, even if it was a bee.

I know she will be disappointed that Princess

Gazania was not rescued.

Abs stands by the storyboard and listens seriously while I explain everything. I tell her all about the dark castle called Chillingsgate Castle, the ride in a basket with a giant eagle owl and the brave gnomes, Basil and Chervil. I tell her I am so, so sorry about not finding Gazania. We both look seriously at the storyboard to see what new clues we have that could help. Everything is arranged carefully but there is nothing that helps with finding the missing Princess. Then I remember the cards and library pockets I found at the back of the library counter.

"Oh Abs," I say slowly, so I don't break her concentration, "I have some clues that I found in the library. I had to draw them on paper but you will see they are symbols, there are no names like on the cards for all the children."

I show Abigail the cards I drew. One with a wolf's head symbol, this is the pocket card and the other with a little crown on it is slipped into the pocket. On the front is the number 398.2. Abs is good at cryptic clues and puzzles. She is one of the smartest girls I know. I am sure she will figure this out and find the answer to where the Princess really is. I feel we are very close now and that the clues are pointing to the library. I watch Abs carefully and wait for her face to light up and then I will know she has found a solution.

I guess she is thinking aloud as she goes over all the clues, the symbols, the numbers, and the library as a part of the crime scene. She puts Miss Sorrel aka Uncle Ru into the scene. I can see she is thinking very hard about something.

Finally, she looks up with a huge grin on her face. "What if," she whispers dramatically. "What if Princess Gazania is being hidden in a book in the library. Like a character in a story. Uncle Ru is keeping her there as part of his evil plan so he can devastate the King and Queen. They feel so miserable they can't fight back and Uncle Ru gets his way and overthrows the King to become king himself. Also with Gazania out of the way there is no other heir to the throne."

Nodding seriously I think about this. What if Gazania is actually in the library and all we need to do is break the code to tell us which book she could be hidden in.

Abs stands up suddenly!

"I've got it!" she says excitedly. "The numbers relate to the coded system for cataloging the library books. We need to find 398.2 and see what books are in that section. I think there is a link to wolves and books as all the wolves on Uncle Ru's games board are standing on books. Did you see any titles?" I shake my head wishing I had been more observant.

"Perhaps it is a story about wolves?" says Abs.

"Or a story with a wolf in it," I add as we both think about stories we have read.

Abs and I discuss the various stories we know with wolves in them and come to the conclusion that it could be one of the traditional fairy tales like the Three Little Pigs, or Peter and the wolf. We dismiss these and think some more. Abs remembers Little Red Riding Hood. It could be the one as there is a girl in the story who goes into a forest and is met by a wolf.

My head nods in agreement. We must look for Little Red Riding Hood. We are a bit confused by the number on the card because it is part of the non-fiction section of the library, but Abs feels it is a part of the clue. When we are sure we have found the right book we make our plan for the way to search inside that book. I believe we will get through the passage of time into the book in the same way as before.

I turn to Abs and am about to say something, when Abs says, with a little tremor in her voice, "Sam, I would really like to find the Princess myself. You see, I personally want to hand back the diary to the Princess."

"What a good idea! I totally agree. Meeting the Princess in a fairytale story like Red Riding Hood is definitely a girl thing!"

I can see Abs is excited to have her own part in the rescue mission and so we agree that we will meet in the library tomorrow at the same time. Abs will find the 398.2 book, it sounds a bit like a prison number! I can cover for Abs in the library while she goes to find and rescue Princess Gazania. There will be a tricky part during the rescue as we try to make a crossing from Little Red Riding Hood's story to Princess Gazania's castle in Gardinia through the herb book.

The next day the library is very quiet. We manage to creep in and get a browsing stick for Abs. She has found that the 398.2 numbers fall under folktales in the social science section.

"Abs, you are so clever, I had no idea how the numbers work in a library," I say. "Maybe you will be a librarian when you grow up!"

We have managed to arrive before Miss Sorrel and we go to look for our storybook. We find a collection of classic fairy tales. It is a book with a number of stories in it. Abs agrees this is a good option and with a very courageous shrug of her shoulders...she lifts her browser towards the book. In a flash, she is gone and I am left staring at the Classical Fairy Tales book in section 398.2.

It feels strange to be without my partner but I know she is the best person to find the Princess Gazania. I just have to wait patiently.

While I am waiting...I think a bit more about the library. Why did Uncle Ru choose the library alongside Gardinia as his crime scene? Two different worlds but both of them able to meet in the library. I think too of the lovely librarian, Miss Jones. She went missing as soon as Miss Sorrel arrived. Where could she be? I am sure she did not leave of her own free will. She loved being in the library.

There are no children in the library right now so I take a few steps towards the library counter. Perhaps there is some information hidden there that could give some clue as to what really happened to Miss Jones. I look carefully behind the muddled up cards and right at the back of the boxes is a brown envelope. Every so often it gives a little wiggle. I wonder what it could be. It is a letter addressed to Miss Jones but the address is crossed out and the word "Bookworm" is written on the front.

Carefully I open the envelope. Inside there is a pupa, the kind that likes to go underground into a dark place waiting to hatch.

I wonder if it is possible that poor Miss Jones was turned into a bookworm and has to pupate before she can get wings and fly. That's the kind of mean trick that a magician could pull.

Suddenly there is a thump in the background and I realize I am not watching section 398.2. I rush back there and sure enough Abs and the Princess are back from the book of fairy tales. They are a bit out of breath and I know Abs is going to tell me the whole story of their escape.

I bow with respect to the Princess and say, "Your highness I am so glad that we have found you and you are safe. The people of Gardinia, especially your parents and of course the gnomes will be thrilled to have you back."

The Princess looks at me and replies, "Samuel Greene, you are a real hero. You have saved the day and me too. I will tell my father that you should receive a knighthood for your bravery. In my father's place I would like to bestow this honor on you right now."

Princess Gazania asks me to kneel in front of her and with her browser stick she taps me on the shoulder to declare my knighthood.

"Arise, Sir Samuel Greene," she says with a very important sounding voice.

" You are a hero to all of Gardinia."

Then she turns to Abigail and thanks her for returning her diary and for all her help in the search and rescue mission. We guide the beautiful Princess towards the Botany section of the library so she can make her entry into Gardinia through the Herb book.

Before she leaves, Gazania says in a solemn voice, "You are not out of danger yet. Uncle Ru specially chose you. He needed a connection to the library through someone who would also make the journey to Gardinia. Someone like you Sam, who would be strong and brave enough to take on this battle against good and evil. Uncle Ru under-estimated you Sam. He thought that he could be smarter than you, but you proved him wrong. He has not finished with you yet. Be on your guard," warns Princess Gazania.

I nod my head and look at Abs. She nods too. We shall be very careful but we hope we have ended Uncle Ru's plans and that Gardinia will return to normal again.

"I don't think you should visit Gardinia until we can be sure Uncle Ru's plans are squashed. I will send you news of how everything is when I am back there," says Princess Gazania. She thanks us once again and with a whoosh from the magical browser stick she disappears into Gardinia.

"Oh Sam, I can just imagine the excitement as she

arrives and Lupa carries her to the castle to be reunited with her parents," says Abs with a huge smile on her face.

It is time to return to the library study area and from there we make our way home. Somehow through all the excitement of rescuing the Princess, I feel we have missed something. I am about to thank Abs and congratulate her on finding and rescuing the Princess when I hear some disturbing noises coming from the front of the library. It sounds like banging and scraping. I wonder what all the fuss is about.

Chapter 12 - Who has the last laugh...

Abigail and I walk slowly to the front of the library, we are not sure of what we will find.

"Surprise! surprise!" – we get such a fright! The noise is coming from the library monitors who are preparing for the end of year library party.

I turn to Abs and say in a hushed whisper, "Whew Abs, I was so worried about that noise. I thought something terrible may be happening. I was thinking that perhaps Uncle Ru knew we had rescued Gazania and he is taking revenge. Thank goodness it is just the furniture being moved for the party!" I sigh with relief again.

"Yes, thank goodness Sam," whispers Abs.

We had both forgotten the party and the presentations for the library awards. We have just got enough time to run home and get changed for the evening.

"Come on Sam, hurry up!" I can hear Abs is excited about the library party.

I don't feel very thrilled about the party, but I know I need to get back. Abs is sure to win the chess trophy. We rush out the door before anyone can call us to help. I race home to change for the evening. Suddenly I remember mom and dad and Uncle Bert were invited too. All the normal school stuff has gone out of my head.

When I get to my room I have a quick look at the storyboard. I can't resist making a few changes as we have rescued Gazania. I am sure when we get news from her...she will tell us that peace has returned to Gardinia and the King and Queen are happy again. There are some unanswered questions but we can meet after the library party and see how to wrap up the investigation.

What a great help Uncle Bert was with so many of the clues.

We need a symbol to represent Princess Gazania, a crown I think. We can put her crown in the picture with the King and Queen. I start to remove Uncle Ru aka Miss Sorrel from the storyboard. I have his symbol, a magician's hat in my hand, but don't know where to put it.

"Ummm..." I say to myself, "we have rescued Gazania but what has happened to Uncle Ru?"

This is a key element of the storyboard that we have not worked out. As I look around for a place to stick the villain, I notice a little figure in the right hand corner of the board. A man in a chair, holding a magnifying glass. Abs and I did not put that figure onto the storyboard. Who could that be? Who else has access to my room? There is no time to think about that so I scrunch Uncle Ru up and throw him in the bin. Then dash out of my room to rush across the road to catch the bus and get to the library party. My parents are coming straight from their work places and meeting me there.

Normally I would have been excited about the awards at the end of the year but this year my Readathon marker did not move off Zero. Thanks to Miss Sorrel aka Uncle Rumex! I try not to get too disappointed, after all, I had a far greater honor given to me in the library by the Princess of Gardinia.

Fortunately, the bus is a bit early and I see Abs standing at the door waiting for me. She signals for to me to follow her to the Botany section of the library. I watch her stand on tiptoes as she reaches for a scroll pushed between the books. News from Gardinia! Wow, that was quick. Perhaps their time zone is not the same as ours. I can't wait to read what Gazania has to say about her return to Gardinia.

Abs and I unroll the scroll. Gazania thanks us again for rescuing her and returning her to the Kingdom of Gardinia. We nod and smile. Then she tells us how wonderful the country is now. Firstly she says her parents, King Costus and Queen Rosemary, were delighted to have their daughter return. They declared a holiday of celebrations to welcome her home. They added their thanks to the letter and enclosed a medal for Sir Samuel the knighted hero and a beautiful necklace for Abs. Abs wrinkled up her nose as she is a bit of a tomboy, but I saw her slip the necklace into a safe place in her pocket. I proudly put the medal around my neck.

There was also a gift from the gnomes addressed to me.

A note said 'Gnomaste' – herbs for peace in the home. The gnomes were packing their best herb seeds and preparing to sell them to raise funds for an animal hospital. Gnomaste, I think that is a wonderful name for a herb collection.

The letter went on to say that Bella Donna had made a complete change to her life. The little gnomes Basil and Chervil had changed her mind about the potions she was making and now she works for good and not evil. Bella Donna has converted her castle into an aviary for birds and changed its name to "Trillingsgate Castle" in honor of all the beautiful bird calls every one hears every day.

She has painted the castle pink and replaced the ugly Gympie trees with beautiful oak trees. She works side by side with the gnomes sharing ideas of medicines and cures for all sorts of ailments. The gray wolves have become her messengers. They deliver medicines all over Gardinia.

Basil organized a group of gnomes to come and seal up the cave of hawk moths so their life cycle would no longer be complete. They would not be able to fly out into the night and cause more damage in Gardinia.

Many bees were rescued and taken back to the gnome's greenhouse to join the Queen bee and start their hives over again. Chervil made a special sweet syrup for the bees to feed on during the winter so they would be ready to fly out and get nectar in the spring. Everything was getting back to normal in Gardinia.

Abs and I looked at each other as we tried to take in all these wonderful things that were happening.

This seems like the perfect happy ending but...where is Uncle Ru? We have forgotten in the excitement of rescuing the Princess that we do not have an answer to that very important question.

Where is Uncle Ru?

He is not in Gardina and we have not seen him in the library...yet.

The sound of clapping in the background reminds us that it is time to get back to the library and the presentations.

Will Miss Sorrel aka Uncle Ru be there disguised as the librarian?

Will we have to play along with his wicked game?

What will we do when we see him face to face?

There are so many unanswered questions. A shiver goes down my spine. The words from Uncle Bert echo in my head – know your enemy.

We feel we know so much about Uncle Ru but at the same time, we know nothing! We don't even know where he is!

Imagine our surprise when we walk round the corner into the library entrance to see Miss Jones standing in front of the parents. Miss Jones, our favorite library teacher is back. She looks beautiful in a bright lime green dress, it flows around her like spectacular butterfly wings. She smiles at everyone and we can see she is glad to be back in the library again.

Miss Jones asks everyone to sit down and then thanks the parents for coming to this evening's presentation. She gives out a few awards and gifts to the library assistants for their help. Then she calls out my name and a great cheer goes up from everyone. I am the winner of the Readathon competition! I stumble up to the front to receive my prize. Miss Jones shakes my hand and whispers in my ear.

"I found your tokens under the library counter, sorry Sam but somehow they were not put on the chart. I sorted that out today and got rid of all the mess under the library counter including a strange looking glass jar full of sand and dried leaves."

I froze at the mention of the jar and leaves. That was the home of Uncle Ru's caterpillar. What had happened to the contents of the jar? Had Miss Jones thrown it away...but where?

I accept my prize and watch Abs receive hers too. She was the chess champ for the year.

There was a lot of cheering and clapping for all the various winners. I am very proud of my award and go across to my parents to share the honor with them. Uncle Bert shakes my hand too.

"Well done, young Sam," he says and gives me a wink.

"How did your project go?" he asks. "Did you finish it?"

I look at Uncle Bert sideways and then I realize the

figure at the bottom of the storyboard is UNCLE BERT! Oh I should have guessed that an experienced forensic entomologist would do more than just give advice from the comfort of an armchair. Uncle Bert knew much more than I realized about the search and rescue mission.

"Uncle Bert, have you been peeking in my room?" I ask, pretending to be furious.

He nods and I can see from the smile on his lips and twinkle in his eyes, that he does not regret sneaking into my room and taking a look at the board. After all, he is a retired detective.

"I have seen all the very good forensic detective work you have done. I know you are the real hero of the day but you have underestimated your enemy."

I wonder what Uncle Bert means by that and I want to ask him...but I am called over to the library counter by Abs and Miss Jones. They want to congratulate me again on winning the Readathon. Mom and Dad come over too and add how proud they are of me.

This is all great but I know I have to find out where Miss Jones took the glass jar and more importantly the contents. She would not have known that the caterpillar in that jar was going to become a Death's Head Hawk moth.

What was Uncle Ru, the master of disguises, planning to do before he disappeared?

Miss Jones is clearly happy to be back in the library. I find the right moment to speak to her and ask her about the jar and its contents. She draws a deep breath and tells me that she threw it outside in the herb garden behind the school kitchen.

"Strange thing happened as I did that, Sam," she adds softly. "There was a funny sort of lumpy, brown thing in the jar. It wriggled into the sand and disappeared before I could find it. I don't know what it was...but I am sure it was alive at the time."

Miss Jones leaves to speak to some parents and I make my way over to Uncle Bert.

Without asking, I know Uncle Bert wants to hear what I have to say. He is already thinking like a forensic entomologist.

I don't want to include Abs in this conversation because I fear it is not what we want to hear.

"Uncle Bert, what does a detective do when the rescue mission is complete. The victim is saved but the key suspect is missing?"

"Well, young Sam," says Uncle Bert. "There is good news and bad news about that kind of situation."

Uncle Bert pauses dramatically and I can see he is enjoying this moment.

"Do you want the good news or the bad news?"

Uncle Bert can see I am in no mood for jokes so he continues. "Well, the good news is that your suspect could have run away and disappeared forever."

I nod and wait for the bad news.

"The bad news is your suspect could have gone into hiding. He will most likely reappear sometime in the future. In the wonderful world of moths, the pupa or chrysalis can bury itself underground and hibernate for a long time. Probably for a year or so and then return to the scene of the crime ready to cause harm to new unsuspecting victims or seek revenge on his enemies."

I am left wondering about Uncle Ru. Did he escape and disappear or is he just in hiding like a wriggly dried-up moth pupa. A Death's Head Hawk moth, bearing the skull tattoo to show off his connection to the insect criminal world. When I get home I will have to get Uncle Ru's symbol out of the bin and put it somewhere until I know the answer to that question.

Everyone is enjoying the library awards party. Abs comes over to me. I can see she wants to share something special with me so I wait at the library counter just in front of the Readathon board.

"Congratulations Sam," she says very sincerely.

"You really were a hero today! From Zero to Hero! Well done, Sir Samuel Greene!"

"Thank you Abs, you were an amazing partner. I would not have managed any of this without your help. We are a good team!"

Abs gives me a big smile and skips off to join the party and I am left with my own thoughts.

Yes, it's great to be called a hero. The library can return to normal and after the party, we will go home for the holidays. I will pack the storyboard away with all the important little figures and symbols used to solve the mystery.

I realize at this moment that it hasn't really finished. Fear runs like a chill down my spine! Uncle Ru has not disappeared. He is disguised somewhere between here and the land of Gardinia. I gave him the connection he needed to our world through the library. Now, what will he be up to next?

I am about to leave the library when Miss Jones calls me over to the library counter. She hands me a card and shrugs her shoulders.

"I don't know what this means," she says, "but it has your initials on it, so maybe you know what it is about?"

S.P.R.O.G. is printed on the outside of the card. On the inside, there is the symbol of a skull and four little words…

Until we meet again!

Book 2 Out Now!

Thank so much for reading Zero to Hero!

If you enjoyed the story, could you please leave a review?

My sincere appreciation.

Katrina x

Some other great books...

This book is dedicated to Christina Withers.

A very special and talented lady.

25571657R00074

Printed in Great Britain
by Amazon